Jeremiah Chaplin

The Evening of Life

Or, light and comfort amid the shadows of declining years

Jeremiah Chaplin

The Evening of Life
Or, light and comfort amid the shadows of declining years

ISBN/EAN: 9783337087814

Printed in Europe, USA, Canada, Australia, Japan

Cover: Foto ©Andreas Hilbeck / pixelio.de

More available books at **www.hansebooks.com**

EVENING OF LIFE;

OR,

LIGHT AND COMFORT

AMIDST THE

SHADOWS OF DECLINING YEARS.

BY

REV. JEREMIAH CHAPLIN, D. D.

THE HOARY HEAD IS A CROWN OF GLORY, IF IT BE FOUND IN THE WAY OF RIGHTEOUSNESS. — Prov. xvi. 31.

A NEW EDITION,

REVISED AND MUCH ENLARGED.

BOSTON:

GOULD AND LINCOLN,

59 WASHINGTON STREET.

NEW YORK: SHELDON AND COMPANY.

CINCINNATI: GEORGE S. BLANCHARD.

1867.

MOTHER'S WAY.

Oft within our little cottage
  As the shadows gently fall,
While the sunl'ght lightly touches
  One sweet face upon the wall—
Do we gather close tog ther,
  And in hushed and tender tone
Ask each o her's full forgiveness
  For the wrong that each has done.
Should you wonder why this custom
  At the ending of the day,
Eye and voice would quickly answer,
  "It was once our mother's way."

If our hom be bright and cheery,
  If it holds a welcome true,
Opening wide its door of greeting
  To the many—not the few;
If we share our father's bounty
  With the needy day by day,
'Tis because our hearts remember
  This was ever mother's way.

Sometimes when our hands grow weary,
  Or our tasks seem very long;
When our burdens lo k too heavy,
  And we deem the right all wrong—
Then we ga'n anew fresh courage,
  And we rise to proudly say:
"Let us do our duty bravely;
  This was our dear mother's way."

Thus we keep her memory precious,
  While we never cease to pray
That at last, when lengthening shadows
  Mark the evening of our day,
They may find us waiti g calmly
  To go home our mother's way.

𝔗𝔬 𝔪𝔶 𝔐𝔬𝔱𝔥𝔢𝔯

THIS SLIGHT OFFERING OF AFFECTION

IS INSCRIBED,

WITH THE FERVENT PRAYER THAT THE

EVENING OF HER LIFE

MAY BE AS HAPPY AS ITS DAY

HAS BEEN USEFUL.

LITTLE LORD JESUS.

Away in a manger, no crib for a
    bed,
The little Lord Jesus laid down his
    sweet head. .
The stars in the bright sky looked
    down where he lay,
The little Lord Jesus asleep on the
    hay.

The cattle are lowing, the baby
    awakes,
But little Lord Jesus, no crying he
    makes.
I love thee, Lord Jesus. Look down
    from the sky
And stay by my cradle till morning
    is high.
                    —Martin Luther.

C E .

This unpretending volume is designed to meet what
is believed to be an actual deficiency. While numerous voices are speaking through the press to the
young and the middle-aged of either sex, those who
have passed the meridian of life are, with rare excep-
tions, left unnoticed—one proof, at least, that among
the virtues of this age is not to be numbered a due
honoring of the hoary head.

But if the young need counsel, the aged need
consolation. With them the day of life is far spent,
and the evening shadows have begun to fall, or are
deepening into night.

We have, therefore, deemed it a pious office as well
as pleasing, to enter, as far as our experience and
observation would enable us, within that world of
thought and feeling, joys and sorrows, hopes and fears,
where the aged dwell, and, in the light of divine
revelation, to look out from their own point of view
upon the Past and Future, that from both we might
gather incentives to the exercise of gratitude and
praise, confidence and hope. And that our offering of
love might be more worthy of their regard, we have
interwoven with our own humble thoughts and affectionate sympathies, the reflections of the wise and

good of the present and other times; in many cases,
the fruit of a long life's experience.

While, in our attempts thus to cheer the evening of
life, we have not overlooked such sources of innocent
happiness as our gracious Father has opened for the
aged as well as for the young, in the present world, it
has been our chief delight to break for them that precious box which is fragrant with the name of Jesus,
and whose sweet perfume is so reviving to the soul.

The hope that this humble volume might be welcomed by those who are approaching or have reached
the autumn and winter of their days, and by others
for their sakes, has made the task of preparation a
pleasant one; and if it shall bring light and comfort
to a single dwelling, or shall lead one impenitent
sinner, even at the eleventh hour, to apply his heart
unto wisdom, it will not have gone forth on its errand
of love in vain.

It may be proper to add, that this volume has been
so prepared that it may be hailed as a friend in the
family of any Christian denomination.

And while it is specially designed for the benefit of
the aged, it may form an appropriate gift from a son
or daughter to parents who have but just passed the
noon of life, as it shows how that evening season,
within whose shades they must soon enter, may be
made bright and peaceful.

To the favor of Him, whose Word so often speaks
the language of tender sympathy for the aged, is this
our labor of love commended, with the prayer that His
blessing may go with it, and cause it to brighten their
pathway to his immediate presence.

PREFACE

NEW, ENLARGED EDITION.

IN now committing this work — truly a work of love — to the Publishers whose well-known names appear upon the title-page, I would anew bespeak for it a kind welcome in the households of the land. I may say, without boasting, that it has been to me a great joy to learn numerous cases where this unpretending volume has come as a messenger of peace. With gratitude to God for his blessing upon it in the past, and in the hope that it may please Him to make it the means of cheering and strengthening yet other hearts, I would now again, and in a form somewhat improved and much enlarged, send it forth on its mission of love.

J. C.

BOSTON, *Dec.* 6, 1858.

1*

CONTENTS.

PROSE.

POETRY.

CONTENTS.

EVENING OF LIFE.

THE HOARY HEAD A CROWN OF GLORY.

WHILE we call old age the winter of our life, we must beware lest we derogate from the bounty of our Maker, and disparage those blessings which He accounts precious; amongst which old age is none of the meanest.

Had He not put that value upon it, would He have honored it with His own style, calling himself the "Ancient of Days?" Would He have set out this mercy as a reward of obedience to himself, "I will fulfil the number of thy days?" and of obedience to our parents, "To live long in the land?" Would He have promised it as a marvelous savor to restored Jerusalem, now become a city of Truth, that "there shall yet old men and old women dwell in the streets of Jerusalem, and every man with his staff in his hand for very age?" Would He else have denounced it as a judgment to over-indulgent Eli, "There shall not be an old man in thy house for ever?" Far be it from us to despise that which God doth honor; and to turn His blessing into a curse.

Yea, the same God who knows best the price of His own favors, as He makes no small estimation of age Himself, so He hath thought fit to call for a high respect to be given to it, out of a holy awe to himself: "Thou shalt rise up before the hoary head, and honor the face of the old man, and fear thy God: I am the Lord." Hence it is that He hath pleased to put together the "ancient" and the "honorable," and has told us that a "hoary head is a crown of glory, if it be found in the way of righteousness;" and lastly, makes it an argument of the deplored estate of Jerusalem that "they favored not the elders."—*Bishop Hall.*

Even to your old age I am He; and even to hoar hairs will I carry you: I have made and I will bear. — *Isaiah* xlvi. 4.

SONNET ON HIS BLINDNESS.

When I consider how my life is spent
Ere half my days, in this dark world and wide,
And that one talent which is death to hide,
Lodged with me useless, though my soul more bent
To serve therewith my Maker, and present
My true account, lest he returning chide;
" Doth God exact day-labor, light denied?"
I fondly ask : But Patience, to prevent
That murmur, soon replies, " God doth not need
Either man's work, or His own gifts ; who best
Bear his mild yoke, they serve him best; His state
Is kingly ; thousands at his bidding speed,
And post o'er land and ocean without rest ;
They also serve who only stand and wait."—*Milton.*

THE OLD MAN'S SOLILOQUY AT THE DIFFERENT SEASONS OF THE YEAR.

SPRING.

THE winter is over, and I am glad to feel the warm sun once more, and the soft south wind that breathes such a balmy fragrance.   As it floats over the land, it whispers gladness and hope to man.   The birds follow its course, warbling their wild-wood notes, and seeking their deserted nests. How sweet the music of the brook that glides noisily down the hill-side, rejoicing to be free again. The children, gay and happy, are running to find the earliest flowers, and manhood, catching the inspiration of the season. seems to resume the freshness of youth. All is life and joy.

But here am I, an old man, in the winter of my days, leaning upon my staff and bending under a load of infirmity. My steps are slow and trembling. Yet I was young once. The memory of those early days is as fresh as ever, and it warms my heart to think of them. Then my spirits were wild and joyous. How changed now! But I would not be young again, noi would I murmur at my decay. A better youth is before me, free from the folly that has stained the past. And somehow I feel now the glow of spring within my heart. Old age has not laid his frosty hand on that. *There* sings a free, gladsome spirit—*there* blooms the flower of hope. As the south wind now blows softly upon my cheek, so my heart feels the warm breathings that come from the land of everlasting spring. There I shall dwell, and be young again. This poor, frail body shall know the vigor and elasticity of youth, fashioned like unto the glorious body of my Saviour. Powerful as a seraph, I shall then rove amid the beauties of that heavenly Paradise. I shall walk with white-robed saints and angels on the banks of the river that flows from the throne, taste the fruit of the tree of life that grows there, and converse upon the high themes of providence and redemption; or else sweep through space to do the will of my Redeemer. No scorching summer shall be there, nor chilling winter, but an eternal spring; ever unfolding new beauty, new fragrance, new melody. No night shall be there, for the Lamb shall be the light thereof. The soft splendor of his glory shall be reflected from every face and every object.

Blessed Spring! I would that thy breeze were now fanning me. But I bow before my Creator's will, cheerfully waiting for my change to come. A few more days in the desert, and then farewell earth, welcome heaven!

SUMMER.

The high sun sends down his hot rays upon the earth. The buds of spring have burst into flowers and fruit, and are fast ripening amid sunshine and shower. The heart of the husband-man rejoices over his luxuriant fields, the promise of a golden harvest.

And yet I linger here—a plant, I trust, in the garden of the Lord. The season leads me to turn my thoughts inward. The spring-time of my religious life has long since passed—the season of my first love to Jesus. A long summer of privileges and means of spiritual growth has followed. The sunshine and dew of heavenly grace have fallen upon me, and with sharp providences the Husbandman has pruned me, that I might bear fruit. How favored among the saints have I been! What precious seasons of communion with my God and Redeemer have I enjoyed! How kindly has he chastened me for my good! What nourishment and comfort have I drawn from the doctrines and promises of the gospel! How sweet has been the communion of the saints! How precious the ordinances of God's house! And my summer is not yet over. I have not, indeed, all the outward means of grace I once enjoyed—infirmity confines me often to my chamber, when my spirit longs for the house of the Lord. But the closet and the

Word, oh! they are still as the summer's sun and shower. There do I find that river, whose streams make glad the city of God; there do I find my Saviour, and sometimes he condescends to smile upon me, and then my poor heart is full to overflowing. I feel the influence of his blessed intercessions, and the sweet breathings of the Spirit. And now and then I have strength to visit the sanctuary, and there I am revived and nourished. Sometimes, too, the Saviour sends one of his dear disciples to cheer me in my solitude, and, oh! what a feast do we enjoy while we talk of Jesus and heaven. Truly the Lord has not been a wilderness unto me. · My sky has not indeed been all sunshine. Sometimes it has been night about me; but then the dew lay upon my roots, and I did not perish. I can remember, too, storms of temptation that swept over me, and threatened my destruction. It seemed then as though all were gone, that I should be uprooted and laid prostrate. Oh! how have my lofty boughs been shaken and broken—how have I been stripped of my pride and beauty, and made to bend before the blast! But He who rides upon the wings of the wind, and directs the storm, caused the tempest to pass oy. The prince of the power of the air was driven back, and again all was calm and bright. These fierce temptations, fearful to remember, served, hrough grace, to fasten my roots more firmly in .he earth, and give me new strength for future assaults. They taught me my weakness, and where alone lay my strength and hope. Thus, even these have been among my means of spiritual growth. And oh, what distressing discoveries have I had of the hidden corruption of my nature. Surely, thought I, I cannot belong to the Lord's garden—I am a cumberer of the ground—it must be said of me, Cut it down. But all this has driven me closer to my Saviour, and revealed to me new glories in his grace. I must reckon these also among my summer privileges. I can bless God for trials and crosses. I would adore the grace that has sanctified them to me. Thanks for the summer that has been granted, with all its clouds, and storms, and darkness. Better than all sunshine. And may it be summer still with my soul, till I die. Let the sun of righteousness still rise upon me, and the dew of heavenly grace fall gently upon me, or I perish. Oh, if it please thee, great God, spare me severe temptations—let not the adversary assail me! But if he be permitted for wise reasons to tempt me, oh! be present with me, and give me a way of escape. Let me not murmur under the rod. Any way, only let me grow in grace, whether in storm or sunshine. When the great harvest-day shall come, may I be found a shock of corn fully ripe.

AUTUMN.

Rich, golden, fruitful autumn! How the sun declines, and sheds a milder radiance. I hear the song of the reaper pouring forth his joy, as I was wont to do. The rich harvest falls around him, and he stands in the midst of smiling plenty.

Bountiful Father! praise to thee for thy benignant providence. Amid these fields, where, so many summers, I have gone forth to my daily toil, seed-time and harvest have come in their unfailing season, according to thy promise. And once more thou crownest the year with thy goodness.

This is the harvest-time, the season of maturity and abundance. How is it with my soul? These green fields shall perish, but my spirit shall survive their desolation. Is it autumn-time with that? Does it exhibit signs of fruitfulness? Do its maturing graces indicate a meetness for the heavenly garner? True, no plant of grace attains its perfection here. The "harvest-home" shall not be sung on earth. But at this late hour should be manifest no doubtful signs of increase and maturity. My long summer of gracious privileges should have made my graces strong and thrifty, and ripened flowers into fruit. As the hour is at hand when the Husbandman shall gather in his harvest, it becomes me to be ready.

Alas! I have to lament my barrenness. When I should flourish like the palm-tree, I am scarce more than a stinted shrub. When I should be laden with fruit, I too much resemble the barren fig-tree. Yet, oh great and good Husbandman, it would be sinful ingratitude to deny what thou hast done for me. Thou hast not permitted the promise of spring to die. Thou hast watched over the seeds of grace; thou hast watered and nourished the tender plants; thou hast kept away the destroying foot and the blighting mildew By the grace of God, I am what I am. I think I care less for the world, sin appears more odious, holiness more lovely, God more glorious, the Saviour more precious, heaven more desirable. Thy word is my delight; thy promises, my stay; the closet, my chosen retreat. I long for more readiness to do and suffer thy will. It pains me that I am no more patient and holy. Oh, to be free from sin, to dwell where every thought will be holy, every breath praise. Is not this the fruit of thy Spirit? It is of thy grace, which has not wrought in vain. In my flesh dwells no good thing, but thy Spirit raises my soul to God. I trust to be accepted through the merits of the Redeemer.

Yet, methinks, there is a sadness in the season. Its influence steals over my spirit and I cannot but weep as a child. Where are the friends of my youth? They have fallen, like leaves, around me. My children—I look for them in vain—they "are gone forth of me, and are not." I am as a tree stripped of its foliage. The moaning wind reminds me that my life is departing, and that I hasten to my account. I think of my imperfection—of my small growth—of the little honor I have brought to my Saviour, and am sad.

But, O Saviour, though I have never loved nor glorified thee as I ought, and have often grieved thee, I must fly to thee. Life is failing, be Thou my strength. Thy blood and righteousness are my only plea. And, oh, make me a more fruitful branch. Affliction and long years have stripped off my leaves; may the sun shine more warmly upon me, and ripen the fruit for heaven! Oh, blessed Paradise, where I shall bring forth fruit in heavenly perfection!

WINTER.

The cold bleak winds of winter are raging without. The snow falls fast, and the trees put on their frosty foliage. This is the old age of the year. Its youth and manhood are past, and now come decrepitude and death. Not a flower can be seen in all the fields, and the warblers have all flown, except the snow-birds that gather crumbs under the window. How cold and drear! The fresh beauty of Spring has left not a trace behind. The old year is dying out.

It is wrapping its drapery of death around it, and preparing to be numbered with the years beyond the flood.

And the winter of my day is come. The frost of age whitens my temples. Like all my fathers, I am descending to the dust. Lord, help me to number my days, and apply my heart unto wisdom. The remnant of my days is but a hand-breadth. May I keep my end in sight. In view of death, how is it with me? Doth death seem terrible, and the grave a place of gloom? Blessed be God, while I sit musing by this cheerful fire, with the precious Bible in my hands, so full of promises, I can say, I would not live always. In this warm room flowers are blooming in mid-winter; so within my heart, amid the frosts of age, the flower of Hope is blossoming for eternity.

The glow of youthful passion is quenched, but instead, the love of Christ burns within me. I feel its blessed warmth. Not things present, nor things to come, can extinguish it. It shall live when my poor body lies in the grave. God himself kindled the flame, and he will allow nothing to quench it. Through the merits of the crucified Redeemer, for me to die will be gain. Come, death—come, life.

Winter is next to spring. Then the flowers will bloom again, and the birds sing as sweetly as ever. And my winter will soon be over, and then an everlasting Spring. Whether another one on earth awaits me, it concerns me not. A brighter and unfading one will open before me. The nearer to death, the nearer to glory. My soul shall be with Jesus. And my body, though it sleep in dust, shall rise, at the resurrection morning, from the corruption of death, in youthful beauty and strength, and then body and spirit shall be companions in glory. Thanks be to God who giveth me the victory through our Lord Jesus Christ.

PRAYER FOR USEFULNESS IN OLD AGE.

SEE you the sun, how majestically and brightly it sheds its parting beams around you? I have heard that the rays of the setting sun produce a most salutary effect on the vegetable word. Oh, that my setting sun, which must soon go down in death, may, during the evening of my days, be more and more blessed in shedding a bene-

ficial light on the trees the Lord hath planted,
and is watering to his glory.—*Rowland Hill.*

THE RETURN OF YOUTH.

My friend, thou sorrowest for thy golden prime,
For thy fair youthful years, too swift of flight;
Thou musest, with wet eyes, upon the time
Of cheerful hopes that filled the world with light;
Years when thy heart was bold, thy hand was strong,
And prompt thy tongue the generous thought to speak,
And willing faith was thine, and scorn of wrong
Summoned the sudden crimson to thy cheek.

Thou lookest forward on the coming days,
Shuddering to feel their shadow o'er thee creep;
A path, thick set with changes and decays,
Slopes downward to the place of common sleep;
And they who walked with thee in life's first stage,
Leave one by one thy side, and, waiting here,
Thou seest the sad companions of thy age—
Dull love of rest, and weariness, and fear.

Yet grieve thou not, nor think thy youth is gone,
Nor deem that glorious season e'er could die;
The pleasant youth, a little while withdrawn,
Waits on the horizon of a brighter sky;
Waits like the morn, but folds her wings and hides,
Till the slow stars bring back her dawning hour;
Waits like the vanished spring, that slumbering bides
Her own sweet time to waken bird and flower.

There shall he welcome thee, when thou shalt stand
On his bright morning hills, with smiles more sweet
Than when at first he took thee by the hand,
Through the fair earth to lead thy tender feet;
He shall bring back, but brighter, broader still,
Life's early glory to thine eyes; again
Shall clothe thy spirit with new strength, and fill
Thy leaping heart with warmer love than then.

Hast thou not glimpses, in the twilight here,
Of mountains where immortal morn prevails?
Comes there not, through their silence, to thine ear
A gentle murmur of the morning gales
That sweep the ambrosial groves of that bright shore,
And thence the fragrance of its blossoms bear,
And voices of the loved ones gone before,
More musical in that celestial air?　　　　*Bryant.*

ZACHARIAH AND ELIZABETH—OR THE AGED PAIR.

BEAUTIFUL is old age when walking in the way of righteousness, and such was the glory that crowned the declining days of the parents of John the Baptist. "They were both righteous before God, walking in all the commandments and ordinances of the Lord blameless."

But doubly beautiful is such old age, when, not pursuing its lonely way, weeping at the remembrance of one with whom that path to glory *had* been trodden, but, alas! smitten down to the dust of death,—it is seen, pressing that path, cheered by the fond companionship of earlier days. And such, too, was the distinguished happiness of Zachariah and Elizabeth. The Providence that had made them one, had kindly continued that union to a good old age. Together do they serve God on earth, together are they waiting for their change to come.

God would seem to have conferred special honor upon pious age, in connexion with that astonishing event, the advent of Jesus. It was no young man to whom was allowed the exalted privilege of giving the first public welcome to the Messiah; but it was Simeon, the just and devout, who had waited for the consolation of Israel. It was no young female, whose voice of praise and thanksgiving blended with Simeon's in the temple over the holy child, but Anna's, the widow of fourscore and four years, who served God with fastings and prayers night and day. And when one is to be raised up as the prophet of the Highest, to go before the Lord in the spirit and power of Elias, beneath whose roof shall he first appear ? Whose, but that of those aged saints before alluded to, whose house had never rung with the glad voice of children ? In their old age shall they have joy and gladness, in the experience of parental love, and in sustaining a most interesting relation to the advent of the Saviour.

Lovely was their life before this event,—passed in the serene beauty of holiness ; but a new glory gilds their path, and new joy fills their hearts, at the fulfilment of the divine promise made through Gabriel. What the Hebrew mother ever deemed her special happiness and honor, but till now denied Elizabeth, is unexpectedly granted her. She embraces a child, and such a child !

It was with delight, but it must have been a strange delight, with which a feeling of awe was blended, that she pressed to her heart this singular child, sanctified even from his birth, the subject of such remarkable predictions, and destined to so sublime a mission. And with what strange feelings must those parents have watched his unfolding childhood, trained as it was under the immediate tuition of the Holy Spirit, and certain,

by God's promise, to expand into a noble man
hood.

Blessed old age! happy home! where domestic
bliss is hallowed by exalted piety, and where we
are taught how even earth may yield pure enjoyment, if only the Spirit of God dwell within us.

The contemplation of this happy, venerable
pair, naturally brings to mind others, whose union,
protracted to a good .old age, has been our
admiration and delight. The evening shadows are, with them, deepening into night, but
they descend hand in hand into the " valley ;"—
they who were one in the spring and summer of
life, are still together in its autumn.

The fall of the year is the season when nature
begins her decline. The chill winds moan
through the trees, the sere and yellow leaf
appears, and the songs of the birds are dying
away. So is it with those whose life is hastening to its close : the beauty of life is faded, the
songs of earlier days are sobered into grave contemplations, and behold, the friends of youth
have fallen like the leaves of the forest. At such a
season of life, it is a blessing to be, not like Abraham when his Sarah was buried from his sight,

or Naomi when bereaved of her husband, but like Zachariah and Elizabeth, leaning upon each other in old age, and cheered by the blessed hope of an eternal union after only a brief separation.

There in the family mansion, in which a third generation may have grown up around them, sit the aged couple—the patriarch of fourscore years, his hoary head a crown of glory; and the venerable matron, the mother perhaps of many sons and daughters. It is pleasing to go in and sit beside them, and engage them in conversation upon the past and future. And you may be almost sure to find them together. In former years, though they loved and lived for each other, their pursuits often called them different ways in the busy world. But now they are never happy except when together. Their enfeebled powers are unequal to any severe toil, and the aged husband, after a short absence, gladly directs his steps homeward to greet her, whose presence has become indispensable to his happiness. How pleasing to witness the childlike simplicity of their affection, displayed in many little acts of kindness toward each other. The schemes which once occupied their minds, at home or abroad have given place to the gentle assiduities of love.

All the scenes through which a long life has led them, whether of prosperity or darkness, have cemented their hearts, and identified their interests more closely together.

Along the path of sorrow they have, perhaps, often walked and wept together, and learned how vain is earth, how true is heaven. The sickness or death of children, when they have mingled their griefs and prayers, the graves where they have laid their dead, the tears they have there shed, the flowers they have there planted, and the visits they have there made; the domestic altar, by which, during long years, morning and evening, parents and children have knelt together; the sanctuary where they have hallowed so many Sabbaths: and the precious revivals, it may be, which they have witnessed, and which have brought the joy of salvation into their own household,—these, and all the other varied scenes of a long pilgrimage have made them inseparably one.

How ready they are to talk over, with themselves or their friends, these past events, and to adore the good hand of the Lord in all the changes that have marked their course since their fortunes became identified.

Of all the friends of their youth, only here and there one remains. The greater part are resting where their own mortal part must soon find its home. Everything admonishes them that life is ebbing, that their sands are almost run. But they do not repine, for they would not live always, and they feel that God has indeed been very merciful to them. They have had their full share of the joys of earth; but they have experienced also its sorrows, and are burdened with its infirmities, and they would gladly soar away and be at rest. They are surrounded, it may be, by those who delight to minister to their comfort, and for this they are thankful; but they have a dearer friend above, better than sons and daughters, infinitely lovely, and they long to be with Him. In Him is their trust, Him they would see and adore How cheerful their spirit, how childlike their faith. And as they have been one in life, so in death they cannot be long divided. Which first shall go they know not: enough, that they shall have the same home for ever.

THE WIFE'S DEATH.

THE death of an old man's wife is like cutting down an ancient oak that has long shaded the family mansion. Henceforth the glare of the world, with its cares and vicissitudes, falls upon the old widower's heart, and there is nothing to break their force or shield him from the full weight of misfortune. It is as if his right hand had withered—as if one wing of his eagle was broken, and every movement that he made brought him to the ground. His eyes are dim and glassy, and when the film of death falls over him, he misses those accustomed tones which might have soothed his passage to the grave.—*Lamartine.*

THE AGED.

I LOVE the aged;—every silver hair
  On their time-honored brows, speak to my heart
In language of the past; each furrow there,
  In all my best affections claims a part;
Next to our God and Scripture's holy page,
Is deepest rev'rence due to virtuous age.

The aged Christian stands upon the shore
  Of Time, a storehouse of experience,
Filled with the treasures of rich heavenly lore;
  I love to sit and hear him draw from thence

Sweet recollections of his journey past,—
A journey crowned with blessings to the last.

Lovely the aged ! when like shocks of corn,
  Full ripe and ready for the reaper's hand,
Which garners for the resurrection morn
  The bodies of the just,—in hope they stand.
And dead must be the heart, the bosom cold,
Which warms not with affection for the old.

Marguerite St. Leon Loud.

LIGHT IN DARKNESS.

God would not hesitate to work wonders in order to turn your sorrow into joy. When in your Gethsemane (for each in his turn enters this garden to sweat blood like the Prince of the just) you shall in your agony have uttered the mournful cry, " Father, let this cup pass from me," the Father might send angels to your assistance, as he did to our generous representative. But Christ needed this assistance, and, thanks to him, we need it not. The angels, who in those dread times will come with a compassionate hand to support our declining head, and wipe the sweat from our brow, are invisible angels, who will not then come for the first time, for they have been long there, and have never quitted us. These invisible angels are faith, hope, and love, if we have detained them beside us by contemplation prayer, and good works; or rather he whom we have detained beside us is God himself; God, whose spirit, as he himself has said, "is in distress in all our distresses." "Though we walk through the valley of the shadow of death, we will fear no evil, for God is with us, his rod and his staff comfort us." Yes, in this very darkness, the blackest of all darkness, in the approaches of death, thou, thyself, O Lord! wilt come to comfort thy poor creatures; thou wilt defend our couch from those visions of terror which ominous appearances and the remembrance of our sins gather around us. Did it seem good to thy wisdom to leave us alone, and without immediate consolation, to perform part of the journey in the darkness of the cavern, it would be on its issue to give a purer and more brilliant light to the sacred day of redemption. The radiant face of our Saviour will enlighten this darkness; we shall not be long in discerning his mild and beneficent countenance; and from that moment, assured and enraptured, we shall feel a sublime joy rise and expand in our soul over our fears, our regrets, and it may be, our remorse. Beside him what can we fear; what can we want? Shall we not be well wherever he is? Can we be perfectly satisfied wherever he is not? Was not the hope which supplied the place of happiness here below, the hope of possessing him? And if it was sweet in this place of exile to suffer with him, what will it be in heaven to reign with him? O revelations, glory, marvels of a Christian death, how great you are and ravishing! Will it ever be possible for us to pay too dearly for them? Is it to pay too much for the death of the righteous to die beforehand, and die daily to ourselves, and hide our life with Christ in the bosom of God? O Lord, teach us this death, in order that we may be capable of the other! O Lord, disrobe us of ourselves, and clothe us with thyself! Make us poor in order that we may be rich! Be our only treasure! Be our only light in the days of happiness, so that thou mayest also be our light in days of mourning, and at the hour of final departure!—*Vinet.*

THE PRESENT AND THE FUTURE.

IT is strange that the experience of so many ages should not make us judge more solidly of the present and of the future, so as to take proper measures in the one for the other. We doat upon this world as if it were never to have an end, and we neglect the next, as if it were never to have a beginning.—*Fenelon.*

BUILD your nest on no tree here; for you see God hath sold the forest to death, and every tree upon which we would rest is ready to be cut down, to the end that we may flee and mount up and build upon the rock.—*Rutherford.*

THE CROSS OF CHRIST.—Christ's cross is the sweetest burden that ever I bore: it is such a burden as wings are to a bird, or sails to a ship, to carry me forward to my harbor.—*Rutherford.*

Children's children are the crown of old men; and the glory of children are their fathers. —*Prov.* xvii. 6

FAITH.

A SWALLOW, in the spring,
Came to our granary, and 'neath the eaves
Essayed to make a nest, and there did bring
Wet earth, and straw, and leaves.

Day after day she toiled,
With patient art, but ere her work was crowned,
Some sad mishap the tiny fabric spoiled,
And dashed it to the ground.

She found the ruin wrought ;
Yet not cast down, forth from the place she flew,
And with her mate fresh earth and grasses brought,
And built her nest anew.

But scarcely had she placed
The last soft·feather on its ample floor,
When wicked hand, or chance, again laid waste
And wrought the ruin o'er.

But still her heart she kept,
And toiled again ;—and, last night hearing calls,
I looked, and lo ! three little swallows slept
Within the earth-made walls.

What truth is here, O man !
Hath Hope been smitten in its early dawn ?
Have clouds o'ercast thy purpose, trust or plan ?
Have Faith, and struggle on !

R. S. S. Andros.

CHRIST AND HIS CROSS.—Hold fast Christ, but take his cross and himself cheerfully; Christ and his cross are not separable in this life, however they part at heaven's door, for there is no room for crosses in heaven; crosses are but the marks of our Lord Jesus, down in this stormy country, or this side death; sorrow and the saints are not married together; or, suppose it were so, heaven will make a divorce.—*Rutherford.*

CHARITY.

'Tis a little thing
To give a cup of water; yet its draught
Of cool refreshment, drained by fevered lips,
May give a shock of pleasure to the frame
More exquisite than when nectarean juice
Renews the life of joy in happiest hours.
It is a little thing to speak a phrase
Of common comfort which by daily use
Has almost lost its sense; yet on the ear
Of him who thought to die unmourned 'twill fall
Like choicest music.—*Talfourd.*

SALVATION BY CHRIST.—People talk about looking back on a well-spent life. I look up to him **who** spent his life gloriously to redeem the life of my precious soul; and there alone I dare to look. I thank God who has kept me from the grosser sins of the world; but there is not a prayer more suitable to my dying lips than that of the publican,—"God be merciful to me a sinner."—*Rowland Hill.*

ROWLAND HILL IN HIS OLD AGE.

When Rowland Hill was far advanced in life, he made a visit to Mrs. Hannah More. In answer to a question from that lady, he informed her that he had vaccinated with his own hand nearly eight thousand persons. One who was present at the interview says: "We talked of everybody, from John Bunyan, to John Locke, and he really showed an excellent discrimination and tact in character. But the most beautiful feature of all was the spirit of love and charity which was eminently conspicuous in this Christian veteran. I cannot express to you how interesting a spectacle it was to see these two already half-beatified servants of their common Lord greeting one another for the first, and probably the last time on this side Jordan, preparatory to the consummation of a unio. and friendship which will last for ever in the region of eternal felicity. I *do* suppose that no two persons in their own generation have done more in their respective ways than Hannah More and Rowland Hill. Both have exceeded fourscore; both retain health and vigor of intellect; both are on the extreme verge of eternity, waiting for the glorious summons, ' Come, ye blessed of my Father.' " He concluded this interesting visit with a fine prayer, which was poured forth in an excellent voice and manner.—*Hannah More's Life.*

CONSOLATION.

PILGRIM burdened with thy sin,
Come the way to Zion's gate,
There, till mercy let thee in,
Knock, and weep, and watch, and wait.
Knock! He knows the sinner's cry;
Weep! He loves the mourner's tears;
Watch! for saving grace is nigh;
Wait—till heavenly light appears.

Hark! it is the bridegroom's voice:
Welcome, pilgrim, to thy rest;
Now within the gate rejoice,
Safe, and sealed, and bought, and blest.

Safe—from all the lures of vice,
Sealed—by signs the chosen know,
Bought—by love, and life the price,
Blest—the mighty debt to owe.

Holy pilgrim ! what for thee
In a world like this remain ?
From thy guarded breast shall flee
Fear, and shame, and doubt, and pain,
Fear—the hope of heaven shall fly,
Shame—from glory's view retire,
Doubt—in certain rapture die,
Pain—in endless bliss expire.—*Crabbe.*

DYING TO SELF.

T_{HE} pious Mr. Berridge says in a letter to Mrs. Wilberforce, when she was in dying circumstances : " Live as near to Jesus as you possibly can, but die, die to *self.* 'Tis a daily work—'tis a hard work. I find myself to be like an insurmountable mountain, or a perpendicular rock that must be overcome ! I've not got over it, not half way over ! This, this is my greatest trial ! Self is like a mountain; Jesus is a sun that shines on the other side of the mountain ; and now and then a sunbeam shines over the top : we get a glimpse, a sort of twilight apprehension of the brightness of the sun ; but *self* must be much more subdued in me before I can bask in the sunbeams of the ever blessed Jesus, or say in everything ' Thy will be done !'

VANITY OF LIFE.

WHAT availeth it to live long, when the improvement of life is so inconsiderable? Length of days, instead of making us better, often increaseth the weight of sin. Would to God that we could live well, only for one day! Many reckon years from the time of their conversion ; but the account of their attainments in holiness is exceedingly small. Therefore, though death be terrible, yet a longer life may be dangerous. Blessed is the man who continually anticipates the hour of his death, and keeps himself in continual preparation for its approach !—*Thomas à Kempis.*

The glory of young men is their strength ; and the beauty of old men is the gray head.—*Prov.* xx. 29.

MEDITATIONS ON DEATH.

IF thou hast ever seen another die, let not the impression of that most interesting sight be effaced from thy heart; but remember, that through the same vale of darkness thou also must pass from this state of existence to the next. When it is morning, think that thou mayest not live till the evening; and, in the evening, presume not to promise thyself another morning. Be, therefore, always ready, and so live, that death may not find thee confounded at its summons. Many die suddenly and unexpectedly: "for in such an hour as ye think not, the Son of man cometh." And when that last hour is come to thee, thou wilt begin to think differently of thy past life, and **be** inexpressibly grieved for thy remissness and inconsideration.—*Thomas à Kempis.*

WARNING TO THE AFFLICTED.—Affliction has a tendency, especially if long continued, to generate a kind of despondency and ill temper: and spiritual incapacity is closely connected with pain and sickness. The spirit of prayer does not necessarily come with affliction. If this be not poured out upon the man, he will, like a wounded beast, skulk to his den and growl there.—*Cecil.*

Christ a Living Saviour.—Christ is not in the heart of a saint, as in a sepulchre, or as a dead Saviour, that does nothing, but as in his temple, and as one that is alive from the dead.— *Pres. Edwards.*

BENEFIT OF AFFLICTION.

The surest way to know our gold is to look upon it and examine it in God's furnace, where he tries it for that end, that we may see what it is. If we have a mind to know whether a building stands strong or no, we must look upon it when the wind blows. If we would know whether that which appears in the form of wheat has the real substance of wheat, or be only chaff, we must observe it, when it is winnowed. If we would know whether a staff be strong, or a rotten, broken reed, we must observe it when it is leaned on, and weight is borne upon it. If we would weigh ourselves justly, we must weigh ourselves in God's scales, that he makes use of to weigh us.—*Pres. Edwards.*

True and False Religion.—The religion of some people is constrained ; they are like people who use the cold bath—not for pleasure, but necessity and their health ; they go in with reluctance, and are glad when they get out. But religion to a true believer is like water to a fish ; it is his element, he lives in it, and he could not live out of it.—*John Newton.*

GLORY OF PRAYER.

WHEN one that holds communion with the skies,
Has filled his urn where these pure waters rise, .
And once more mingles with us, meaner things,
'Tis e'en as if an angel shook his wings ;
Immortal fragrance fills the circuit wide,
That tells us whence the treasure is supplied.—*Cowper.*

THE PATRIARCH.

BEHOLD a patriarch of years, who leaneth on the staff of
    religion ;
His heart is fresh, quick to feel, a bursting fount of generosity ;
He, playful in his wisdom, is gladdened in his children's glad-
    ness.
He, pure in his experience, loveth in his son's first love :
Lofty aspirations, deep affections, holy hopes are his delight ;
His abhorrence is to strip from life its charitable garment of
    ideal.
The shrewd world laughed at him for honesty, the vain world
    mouthed at him for honor,
The false world hated him for truth, the cold world despised
    him for affection.

Still, he kept his treasure, the warm and noble heart,
And in that happy old man survive the child and lover.

Tupper.

THE BIBLE.—I will answer for it, the longer you read the Bible, the more you will like it; it will grow sweeter and sweeter; and the more you get into the spirit of it, the more you will get into the spirit of Christ.—*Romaine.*

TRIALS.—Outward attacks and troubles rather fix than unsettle the Christian, as tempests from without only serve to root the oak faster; whilst an inward canker will gradually rot and decay it.—*H. More.*

SALMASIUS.

SALMASIUS was a man of most extraordinary abilities, his name resounded through Europe, and his presence was earnestly sought in different nations. When he arrived at the evening of life, he acknowledged that he had too much, and too earnestly engaged in literary pursuits. "O!" said he, " I have lost an immense portion of time; time, that most precious thing in the world! Had I but one year more, it should be spent in studying David's Psalms and Paul's Epistles.

Oh! sirs," said he to those about him, " mind the world less, and God more. 'The fear of the Lord, that is wisdom ; and to depart from evil, that is understanding.'"—*Pike.*

BLESSEDNESS OF HEAVEN.

On a certain day known only to the Lord, the reign of the Prince of Peace will commence ; when instead of the vicissitudes of day and night, joy and sorrow, that are now known, there shall be uninterrupted light, infinite splendor, unchangeable peace, and everlasting rest. Then thou wilt no longer say, " Who shall deliver me from the body of this death ?" nor exclaim, " Woe is me that my pilgrimage is prolonged !" for " death shall be swallowed up in victory," and " the corruptible will have put on incorruption." Then " all tears shall be wiped from thy eyes," and all sorrow taken from thy heart ; and thou shalt enjoy perpetual delight in the lovely society of angels, and the " spirits of the just made perfect." - *Thomas à Kempis.*

O was it possible for thee to behold the unfading brightness of those crowns which the blessed wear in heaven ; and with what triumphant glory they, whom the world once despised, and thought unworthy of life itself, are now invested; verily, thou wouldst humble thyself to the dust, and rather choose to be inferior to all men, than superior even to one; instead of sighing for the perpetual enjoyment of the pleasures of this life, thou wouldst rejoice in suffering all its afflictions for the sake of God; and wouldst count it great gain to be despised and rejected as nothing among men.—*Thomas à Kempis.*

ELLIOT IN HIS OLD AGE.

On the day of his death, in his eightieth year, Elliot, "the apostle of the Indians," was found teaching the alphabet to an Indian child at his bed-side. "Why not rest from your labors now?" said a friend. "Because," said the venerable man, "I have prayed to God to render me useful in my sphere; and he has heard my prayers; for now that I can no longer preach, he leaves me strength enough to teach this poor child his alphabet."

The best prayers have often more groans than words.—*Bunyan.*

LIVE IN VIEW OF DEATH.

So live, that when thy summons comes to join
The innumerable caravan, that moves
To the pale realms of shade, where each shall take
His chamber in the silent halls of death,
Thou go not, like the quarry slave at night,
Scourged to his dungeon ; but, sustained and soothed
By an unfaltering trust, approach thy grave
Like one who wraps the drapery of his couch
About him, and lies down to pleasant dreams.—*Bryant.*

PRAYER.

I have seen a lark rising from his bed of grass and soaring upwards, singing as he rises, in hopes to get to heaven and climb above the clouds; but the poor bird was beaten back with the loud sighing of an eastern wind, and his motion made irregular and inconstant, descending more at every breath of the tempest than all the vibrations of his wings served to exalt him, till the little creature was forced to sit down and pant, and stay till the storm was overpast; and then it made a prosperous flight; for then it did rise and sing as if it had learned music and motion from some angel as he passed some time through the air. So is the prayer of the good man when agitated by any passion. He fain would speak to God, and his words are of the earth, earthy; he would look to his Maker, but he could not help seeing also that which distracted him, and a tempest was raised and the man overruled; his prayer was broken and his thoughts were troubled, and his words ascended to the clouds, and the wandering of his imagination recalled them, and in all the fluctuating varieties of passion they are never like to reach God at all. But he sits him down and sighs over his infirmity, and fixes his thoughts upon things above, and forgets all the little vain passages of this life, and his spirit is becalmed, and his soul is even and still, and then it softly and sweetly ascends to heaven on the wings of the Holy Dove, and dwells with God, till it returns, like the useful bee, loaded with a blessing and the dew of heaven.—*Jeremy Taylor.*

CLOUDY DAYS.

A BLACK cloud makes the traveller mend his pace, and mind his home; whereas a fair day and a pleasant way waste his time, and that stealeth away his affections in the prospect of the country. However others may think of it, yet

3*

I take it as a mercy, that now and then some clouds come between me and my sun, and ma..y times some troubles do conceal my comforts; for I perceive, if I should find too much friendship in my inn, in my pilgrimage, I should soon forget my father's house and my heritage.—*Lucas.*

THE CHRISTIAN ON EARTH AND IN HEAVEN.

Sometimes I look upon myself, and say, "Where am I now?" and do quickly return answer to myself again, "Why, I am in an evil world, a great way from heaven, in a sinful world, among devils and wicked men; sometimes benighted, sometimes beguiled, sometimes fearing, sometimes hoping, sometimes breathing, sometimes dying." But then I turn the tables, and say, "But where shall I be shortly? Where shall I see myself anon after a few times more have passed over me?" and when I can but answer this question thus: "I shall see myself with Jesus Christ;" this yields glory, even glory to one's spirit now.—*Bunyan.*

SONNET, "ADIEU, MY YOUTH!"

[FROM THE ITALIAN.]

Adieu, my youth! without one sigh adieu!
Deceits, enchantments, struggles, longings, dreams,

Delusions, follies—(no light load meseems !)—
Take all ! Cast to the winds thy retinue.
The mind swollen out with mists which hide from view
A host of daring thoughts that scorn the wise—
And wandering love, fresh arrows, as he flies,
Infixing still—and hatreds fierce, though few !
An eve serene and still, my soul, sore tried
With earthly warfare, courts. My youth, adieu !
But not adieu forever. Yet again,
I trust to meet—to dwell in thee—not vain,
And frail, and fallen, as now, but born anew,
Stainless, redeemed, immortal, glorified !

DEATH OF ROBERT BRUCE.

MR. ROBERT BRUCE, the morning before he died, being at breakfast, having, as he used, taken an egg, said to his daughter, "I think I am yet hungry ; you may bring me another egg." But having mused awhile, he said, " *Hold, daughter hold, my Master calls me.*" With these words his sight failed him ; on which he called for the Bible, and said, " Turn to the eighth chapter of he Romans, and set my finger on the words,—
I am persuaded that neither death, nor life, &c., shall be able to separate me from the love of God, which is in Christ Jesus my Lord.'"
When this was done, he said, " Now is my fin-

ger upon them ?" Being told that it was, he added, " Now, God be with you, my dear children : I have breakfasted with you, and shall sup with my Lord Jesus Christ this night;" and then he expired.—*Whitecross's Anecdotes.*

THE EVENING OF LIFE.

THERE is a healing in the bitter cup. God takes away or removes from us those we love, as hostages of our faith (if I may so express it) ; and to those who look forward to a re-union in another world, where there will be no separation and no mutability, except that which arises from perpetual progressiveness, the evening of life becomes more delightful than the morning, and the sunset offers brighter and lovelier visions than those which we build in the morning clouds, and which appear before the strength of the day. And faith is that precious alchemy which trans-mutes grief into joy ; or, rather, it is the pure and heavenly euphrasy, which clears away the film from our mortal sight, and makes affliction appear what it really is, a dispensation of mercy.

GOD'S MERCY.

THE mercy of God is a huge ocean ; from eternal ages it dwelt round about the throne of God, and it filled all that infinite distance and space that hath no measures but the will of God ; until God, desiring to communicate that excellency, created angels, that he might have persons capable of huge gifts ; and man, who he knew would need forgiveness. For so the angels, our elder brothers, dwelt for ever in the house of their Father, and never broke his commandments ; but we, the younger, like prodigals, forsook our Father's house, and went into a strange country, and followed stranger courses, and spent the portion of our nature, and forfeited all our title to the family, and came to need another portion. For, ever since the fall of Adam, who, like an unfortunate man, spent all that a wretched man could need, or a happy man could have, our life is repentance, and forgiveness is all our portion ; and though angels were objects of God's bounty, yet man only is, in proper speaking, the object of his mercy ; and the mercy that dwelt in an infinite circle became confined to a little ring, and dwelt here below ; and here shall dwell below, till it hath carried all

God's portion up to heaven, where it shall reign in glory upon our crowned heads for ever and ever!—*Jeremy Taylor*.

THE GOODNESS OF GOD THE SOLACE OF THE AGED.

See how old age spoils the relish of outward delights, in the example of Barzillai, 2 Sam. xix. 35; but it makes not this (the graciousness of God) distasteful. Therefore the Psalmist prays, that when other comforts forsake him and wear out, when they ebb from him, and leave him on the sand, this may not: that still he may feed on the goodness of God. "Cast me not off in old age, forsake me not when my strength faileth." It is the continual influence of his graciousness that makes them grow like "cedars of Lebanon," that makes them "bring forth fruit in old age, and to be still fat and flourishing; to show that the Lord is upright," as it is there added, that he is (as the word imports) *still like himself*, and his goodness ever the same.—*Leighton*.

THE WHOLE FAMILY IN HEAVEN AND EARTH.

"The whole family in heaven and earth." The difference betwixt us and them is, not that we are really two, but one body in Christ, in divers places. True, we are below stairs, and they above; they in their holiday, and we in our working-day clothes; they in harbor, but we in the storm; they at rest, but we in the wilderness; they singing, as crowned with joy, we crying, as crowned with thorns. But we are all of one house, one family, and are all children of one Father.—*Bunyan*.

PSALM OF LIFE.

Tell me not in mournful numbers,
    Life is but an empty dream!
For the soul is dead that slumbers,
    And things are not what they seem.

Life is real! Life is earnest!
    And the grave is not its goal;
"Dust thou art, to dust returnest,"
    Was not spoken to the soul.

Not enjoyment, and not sorrow,
    Is our destined end or way;
But to act, that each to-morrow
    Find us farther than to-day.

Art is long, and Time is fleeting,
    And our hearts, though stout and brave,
Still, like muffled drums, are beating
    Funeral marches to the grave.

In the world's broad field of battle,
    In the bivouac of Life,
Be not like dumb, driven cattle !
    Be a hero in the strife !

Trust no Future, howe'er pleasant !
    Let the dead Past bury its dead !
Act ;—act in the living Present !
    Heart within, and God o'erhead !

Lives of great men all remind us
    We can make our lives sublime,
And, departing, leave behind us
    Footprints on the sands of time.

Footprints, that perhaps another,
    Sailing o'er life's solemn main,
A forlorn and shipwrecked brother,
    Seeing, shall take heart again.

Let us, then, be up and doing,
    With a heart for any fate ;
Still achieving, still pursuing,
    Learn to labor and to wait.   *Longfellow.*

THINGS TO REMEMBER.—Be often remembering what a blessed thing it is to be saved, to go to heaven, to be made like angels, and to dwell with God and Christ to all eternity.—*Bunyan.*

SANCTIFICATION.

In the sanctified heart, "every mountain is brought low, and every valley is filled." Everything within us which exalts itself in the pride and love of nature, is cast out or abased.

And again, in the sanctified soul "every valley is filled," by being occupied with God and with Jesus Christ only It is a great truth, that God does not and cannot fill the soul with himself, until he first empties it of everything which is not himself. The mountain, which may be regarded as another name for the exaltation of nature, must first be brought low, and must be cast out. And into this *void* or valley, where a man may be said to possess himself without himself, God enters and fills it up. Truth takes the place of error. Holy dispositions take the place of unholy dispositions; and God, who embodies in himself all truth and all holiness, and who always creates that immortal image which bears his own likeness, can never be absent where true and holy dispositions exist. In such dispositions, of which he is the true light and life, he not only is, but *must* be. Without God in them, they cannot exist. They are God's home.

The subjection of human selfishness by holy love, and the subjection of the human will by union with the divine will;—it is these which constitute a truly renovated nature, and which, because they thus constitute the same nature with Christ's nature, may be said to make *Christ within* us.   Christ, in some future years, will come visibly in the clouds of heaven.   Oh! let us labor for his *present* coming; not for a Christ in the clouds, but for a Christ in the affections; not for a Christ seen, but for a Christ felt; not for a Christ outwardly represented, but for a Christ inwardly realised.—*Madame Guyon.*

PRAYER FOR SANCTIFICATION.

O Holy Spirit, a Spirit of love! let me ever be subjected to thy will; and as a leaf is moved before the wind, so let my soul be influenced and moved by the breath of thy wisdom.   And as the impetuous wind breaks down all that resists it, even the towering cedars which stand in opposition; so may the Holy Ghost, operating within me, smite and break down everything which opposes him.—*Madame Guyon.*

DYING WORDS OF PAYSON.

Dr. Payson in his last illness once said: "I have suffered twenty times,—yes, to speak within bounds, twenty times as much as I could in being burnt at the stake, while my joy in God so abounded, as to render my sufferings not only tolerable, but welcome. The sufferings of this present time are not worthy to be compared with the glory that shall be revealed. God is my all in all. While he is present with me, no event can in the least diminish my happiness; and were the whole world at my feet, trying to minister to my comfort, they could not add one drop to the cup." On another occasion he said, "Death comes every night and stands at my bedside in the form of terrible convulsions, every one of which threatens to separate the soul from the body. These continue to grow worse and worse, until every bone is almost dislocated with pain, leaving me with the certainty that I shall have it all to endure again the next night. Yet while my body is thus tortured, the soul is perfectly happy, perfectly happy and peaceful, more happy than I can possibly express to you. I lie here, and feel these convulsions extending higher and higher, but my soul is filled with joy unspeakable. I seem to swim in a flood of glory, which God pours down upon me."—*Payson's Life.*

THE AFFLICTED BELIEVER.

WE may compare an afflicted believer to a man that has an orchard laden with fruit, who, because the wind has blown off the leaves, sits down and weeps. If one asks, "What do you weep for?" "Why, my apple leaves are gone." "But have you not your apples left?" "Yes." "Very well, then do not grieve for a few *leaves* which could only hinder the ripening of your fruit."—*Cecil.*

BENEFIT OF AFFLICTION.

I HAVE before me two stones, which are an imitation of precious stones. They are both perfectly alike in color; they are of the same water, clear, pure, and clean; yet there is a marked difference between them as to their lustre and brilliancy. One has a dazzling-brightness, while the other is dull, so that the eye passes over it, and derives no pleasure from the sight. What can be the reason of the difference? It is this: the one is cut in but a few *façets;* the other has ten times as many. These façets are produced by a very violent operation. It is requisite to cut, to smooth, and polish. Had these stones been indued with life, so as to have been capable of feeling what they underwent, the one which has received eighty *façets,* would have thought itself very unhappy, and would have envied the fate of the other, which, having received but eight, had undergone but a tenth part of its sufferings. Nevertheless, the operation being over, it is done for ever; the difference between the two stones always remains strongly marked; that which has suffered but little, is entirely eclipsed by the other, which alone is held in estimation and attracts attention. May not this serve to explain the saying of our Saviour, whose words have reference to eternity? "Blessed are those who mourn, for they shall be comforted,"—blessed, whether we contemplate them apart, or in comparison with those who have not passed through so many trials. Oh! that we were always able to cast ourselves into his arms, like little children; to draw near to him, like young lambs, and ever to ask of him, patience, resignation, an entire surrender to his will, faith, trust, and heartfelt obedience to the commands which he gives to those who are willing to be his disciples. "The Lord will wipe away tears from off all faces." —*Oberlin.*

PEACE OF MIND.

A friend once asked Prof. Francke, who founded the Orphan-house at Halle, how he maintained so constant a peace of mind; the benevolent and good man replied,—"By stirring up my mind a hundred times a day. Wherever I am, whatever I do, I say,—'Blessed Jesus, have I truly a share in thy redemption? Are my sins forgiven? Am I guided by thy spirit? Thine I am—wash me again and again.' By this constant converse with Jesus I have enjoyed serenity of mind, and a settled peace in my soul."

PRAYER OF THE AGED.

But while from one extreme thy power may keep
  My erring frailty, O, preserve me still
From dullness, nor let cold indifference steep
  My senses in oblivion : if the thrill
Of earthly bliss must sober, as it will

And should, when earthly things to heavenly yield,
I would have feelings left time cannot chill;
That while I yet can walk through grove or field,
I may be conscious there of charms by thee revealed.
And when I shall, as soon or late I must,
Become infirm, in age if I grow old,
Or sooner, if my strength should fail its trust,
When I relinquish haunts where I have strolled
At morn or eve, and can no more behold
Thy glorious works, forbid me to repine;
Let memory still their loveliness unfold
Before my mental eye, and let them shine
With borrowed light from thee—for they are thine.

Barton.

TRUE WEALTH.—The wealth of a man is the number of things which he loves and blesses which he is loved and blessed by.—*Carlyle.*

EFFECTS OF GRACE.—The dispensation of grace is to some little more than a continual combat with corruptions; so that, instead of advancing, a man seems to be just able to preserve himself from sinking. A boat, with the full tide against it, does well if it can keep from driving back, and must have strong force indeed to get forward. We must estimate grace by the opposition it meets with.—*Cecil.*

THE AGED COMFORTER.

Tis true that more than fourscore years have bowed thy beauty
    low,
And mingled with thy cup of life full many a dreg of woe ;
But yet thou hast a better charm than bloom of youth hath
    found—
A balm within thy chastened heart to heal another's wound.

Sigourney.

ANECDOTE OF DR. COGSWELL.

An affecting anecdote is related of Dr. Cogs-
well, a faithful minister in Hartford, Conn., who
died at the age of eighty-nine. It shows "the
ruling passion strong in death." During his last
illness he forgot his dearest friends, and even his
own name. When asked if he remembered his
son (with whom he lived, and to whom he was
much attached), he replied, "I do not recollect
that ever I had a son;" but when asked if he
remembered the Lord Jesus Christ, he revived at
once, exclaiming, "Oh ! yes, I do remember him ,
he is my God and my Redeemer !"

THE FLIGHT OF TIME.

THE dial-plate warns you that minutes are fleeting,
Each pulse but wears out the heart that is beating ;
Each tick of the clock is ever repeating—
"Up and be doing ! for Night draweth on !"

Knickerbocker (Mag.)

TRUST IN GOD.

EXAMPLES of the loving-kindness of God to his aged servants have been recorded in his word for our learning ; that believers, if God by his providence should bring them to old age, might be encouraged to trust in the God of Abraham, Isaac, and Jacob, with such a confidence of their hearts as not to doubt of the divine truth or of the divine power. Whatever he was to them, he is the same to us—our God as well as theirs—our covenant God, engaged to glorify both body and soul : on whom we are commanded to cast all our cares and concerns in extreme old age. If what is of nature be failing, what is of grace cannot. If the life of sense be dying, the life of faith should flourish the more. It is a life that cannot die; for the branches thrive and bring forth fruit in their old age, not of themselves, but because they are ingrafted into the heavenly vine, in which they live for ever. "I am the vine (says Jesus), ye are the branches; he that abideth in me, and I in him, the same bringeth forth much fruit: for without me ye can do nothing." But through his spirit strengthening you, he will make you bud and flourish, and fill the face of the world with fruit. He will so fill you with the fruits of righteousness, which are through Christ Jesus, to the glory and praise of God, that your last days will be your best days.—*Romaine.*

SAYINGS OF JOHN NEWTON.

Two or three years before the excellent John Newton's death, when his sight was become so dim, that he was no longer able to read, an aged friend and brother in the ministry called on him, to breakfast. Family prayer succeeding, the portion of Scripture for the day was read to him. It was taken from Bogatzky's Golden Treasury: "By the grace of God I am what I am." It was the pious man's custom, on these occasions, to make a short familiar exposition of the passage read. After the reading of this text, he paused for some moments, and then uttered the following affecting soliloquy :—"I am not what I *ought* to be. Ah! how imperfect and deficient. I am not what I *wish* to be. I abhor what is evil, and I would cleave to what is good. I am not what I *hope* to be: soon, soon I shall put off mortality, and with mortality all sin and imperfection   Yet though I am not what I *ought* to be, nor what I *wish* to be, nor what I *hope* to be, I can truly say I am not what I *once* was,—a slave to sin and Satan; and I can heartily join with the apostle, and acknowledge, ' By the grace of God I am what I am.' Let us pray."— *Whitecross' Anecdotes.*

THE CHRISTIAN PILGRIMAGE.

THE Christian's fellowship with God is rather a habit than a rapture. He is a pilgrim who has the habit of looking forward to the light before him; he has the habit of not looking back; he has the habit of walking steadily in the way whatever be the weather, and whatever the road. These are his habits, and the Lord of the way is his Guide Protector, Friend, and Felicity.— *Cecil.*

THE LAND OF BEULAH

Were I to adopt the figurative language of Bunyan, I might date this letter from the land of Beulah, of which I have been for some weeks a happy inhabitant. The celestial city is full in my view. Its glories beam upon me, its breezes fan me, its odors are wafted to me, its sounds strike upon my ears, and its spirit is breathed into my heart. Nothing separates me from it but the river of death, which now appears but an insignificant rill, that may be crossed at a single step, whenever God shall give permission. The sun of righteousness has been gradually drawing nearer and nearer, appearing larger and brighter as he approached, and now he fills the whole hemisphere, pouring forth a flood of glory, in which I seem to float like an insect in the beams of the sun; exulting, yet almost trembling while I gaze on this excessive brightness, and wondering, with unutterable wonder, why God should deign thus to shine upon a sinful worm. A single heart and a single tongue seem altogether inadequate to my wants: I want a whole heart for every separate emotion, and a whole tongue to express that emotion.—*Payson*. (*Letter to a sister*.)

LET not your heart be troubled : ye believe in God, believe also in me. In my Father's house are many mansions : if it were not so, I would have told you. I go to prepare a place for you. And if I go to prepare a place for you, I will come again and receive you unto myself; that where I am, there ye may be also.—*John* xiv. 1, 2, 3.

THE BRUISED REED.

" A BRUISED reed will he not break." Perhaps the imagery may be derived from the practice of the ancient shepherds, who were wont to amuse themselves with the music of a pipe of reed or straw ; and when it was bruised they broke it, or threw it away as useless. But the bruised reed shall not be broken by this divine shepherd of souls. The music of broken sighs and groans is indeed all that the broken reed can afford him : the notes are but low, melancholy, and jarring ; and yet he will not break the instrument, but he will repair and tune it. till it is fit to join in the

concert of angels on high; and even now is
humble strains are pleasing to his ears.—*Pres
Davies.*

THE SHORE OF TIME.

Alone I walked the ocean strand;
A pearly shell was in my hand:
I stooped and wrote upon the sand
My name—the year—the day.
As onward from the spot I passed
One lingering look behind I cast:
A wave came rolling high and fast,
And washed my lines away.

And so, methought, 'twill shortly be
With every mark on earth from me;
A wave of dark oblivion's sea
Will sweep across the place,
Where I have trod the sandy shore
Of time, and been to be no more;
Of me—my day—the name I bore,
Nor leave nor track, nor trace.

And yet, with Him who counts the sands,
And holds the waters in his hands,
I know a lasting record stands
Inscribed against my name,
Of all this mortal part has wrought;
Of all this sinking soul has thought;
And from these fleeting moments caught
For glory, or for shame.—*Hannah F. Gould.*

SAINTS OF DIFFERENT DEGREES.

God has saints of several degrees, and some
of them have more communion with him than
others; from among the multitude he chose
twelve to be with him; from among the twelve
he chose three, Peter, James, and John, who
were of the privy council; from among the three
he chose out John, as his bosom-favorite, of
whom it is said five times in John's gospel,
that "he was the disciple whom Jesus *loved.*"

So now, at this day, God has his "babes," who
live upon milk; he has "children" also, who
know their Father, and are assured of his love;
moreover, he has his "young men," who go out
to war, and fight the Lord's battles victoriously;
and he has "fathers" in Israel, who abound in
grey-headed experience and wisdom; for they
knew him from the beginning, and they remember his words. It is a great mercy to be one of
God's "little ones," yea, the least of all, to be a
star, though not of the first magnitude; to be a
disciple, though not a John; not one of the three,
nor one of the twelve, nor one of the seventy. It
is a mercy to be new-born, to be taken into the
family of God, and household of faith. But to

grow up to a perfect stature, to be a man in Christ Jesus! O how great a mercy! Lord, thou knowest my desires; perfect that which concerns thy servant, yea, that which concerns all thy servants.—*Bogatzky.*

WE have not a high-priest who cannot be touched with the feeling of our infirmities, but was in all points tempted like as we are, yet without sin. Let us therefore come boldly unto the throne of grace, that we may obtain mercy, and find grace to help in time of need.—*Heb.* iv. 15, 16.

THE FATHER'S DEATH.

THERE are children round their father's bed,
And his last farewell is given—
There's joy in their grief—a blessing shed,
At once from their sire and heaven.
Deep is the peace that reigns around,
Where the faithful in his faith is crowned,
For the Holiest of holies is o'er his bed—
The Spirit of him who wakes the dead.—*Stebbing.*

STUDY OF THE BIBLE.

IF thou complainest nothing remains on thy memory, therefore thou thinkest as good to give over reading as thus continually to pour water into a sieve; this should rather put thee on a more frequent study of the Scripture, than discourage thee from it. A vessel set under the fall of a spring cannot leak faster than it is supplied Scripture truths, when they do not enrich the memory, may yet purify the heart. Such is the irresistible force of the word, the Spirit often darts it through us as it seems but a flash of lightning, and it is gone; yet it may melt our hard hearts when it leaves no impression on our memories.—*Bishop Hopkins.*

TRUST IN GOD.

" By thy grace
The particle divine remained unquenched;
And 'mid the wild weeds of a rugged soil,
Thy bounty caused to flourish deathless flowers
From Paradise transplanted; wintry age
Impends; the frost will gather round my heart;
If the flowers wither, I am worse than dead!
Come, labor, when the worn-out frame requires
Perpetual sabbath; come, disease and want,
And sad exclusion through decay of sense;
But leave me unabated trust in thee—
And let thy favor, to the end of life,

> Inspire me with ability to seek
> Repose and hope among eternal things—
> Father of heaven and earth! and I am rich,
> And will possess my portion in content."—*Worasworth.*

CONSOLATION FOR SUFFERERS.—If your Lord call you to suffering, be not dismayed; there shall be a new allowance of the King for you, when ye come to it: one of the softest pillows Christ hath is laid under his witnesses' head, though often they set down their feet among thorns.—*Rutherford.*

AFFLICTION THE PORTION OF THE SAINTS.

IT is not wisdom for us to think that Christ and the gospel will come and sit down at our fireside: nay, but we must go out of our warm houses, and seek Christ and his gospel. We must set our face against what may befall us, in following on through the briers. Our soft nature would be borne through the troubles of this miserable world in Christ's arms; and it is his wisdom, who knoweth our mould, that his children go wet-shod and cold-footed to heaven. Oh! how sweet a thing it were for us to learn

to make our burdens light, by framing our hearts
to the burden, and making our Lord's will a
law! I find Christ and his cross not so ill to
please, nor yet such troublesome guests as men
call them: ere long, our Master will bring this
whole world out before the sun and daylight, in
their blacks and whites. Happy are they who
are found watching; our sand-glass is not so
long as we need to weary; time will eat away
and root out our woes and sorrow; our heaven
is in the bud, and growing up to an harvest.
Why then should we not follow on, seeing our
span-length of time will come to an inch?
Therefore I commend Christ to you as the staff
of your old age; let him now have the rest of
your days.

Think not much of a storm upon the ship that
Christ saileth in; there shall no passenger fall
overboard, but the crazed ship and the sea-sick
passengers shall come to land safe.—*Rutherford.*

THE days of our years are threescore years
and ten; and if by reason of strength they be
fourscore years, yet is their strength labor and
sorrow; for it is soon cut off, and we fly away.

. . . So teach us to number our days, that we may apply our hearts unto wisdom. — *Psalm* xc. 10, 12.

Like as a father pitieth his children, so the Lord pitieth them that fear him. For he know eth our frame; he remembereth that we are dust. — *Psalm* ciii. 13, 14.

Whom the Lord loveth he chasteneth, and scourgeth every son whom he receiveth. — *Heb.* xii. 6.

THE ANGEL OF PATIENCE.

To weary hearts, to mourning homes,
　God's meekest angel gently comes:
No power has he to banish pain,
　Or give us back our lost again;
And yet in tenderest love, our dear
　And Heavenly Father sends him here.

There's quiet in that angel's glance;
　There's rest in his still countenance!
He mocks no grief with idle cheer,
　Nor wounds with words the mourner's ear;
But ills and woes he cannot cure,
　He kindly trains us to endure.

Angel of Patience ! sent to calm
  Our feverish brows with cooling palm ;
To lay the storms of hope and fear,
  And reconcile life's smile and tear ;
The throbs of wounded pride to still,
  And make our own our Father's will.

Oh ! thou who mournest on thy way,
  With longings for the close of day ;
He walks with thee, that angel kind,
  And gently whispers, "Be resigned :
Bear up, bear on, the end shall tell
  The dear Lord ordereth all things well !"

J. G. Whittier.

Loss of Children.—Let your children be as flowers borrowed from God ; if the flowers die or wither, thank God for a summer's loan of them, and keep good neighborhood, to borrow and lend with him.—*Rutherford.*

HOPE AMID TRIALS.

Let my Lord Jesus weave my span-length o! time with white and black, weal and woe, as warp and woof in one web ; and let the rose be neighbored with the thorn ; yet Hope that maketh not ashamed, hath written a letter to the mourners in Zion, that it shall not be long so When we are over the water, Christ shall cry down crosses, and hell, and death, and sin, and sorrow, and up glory, life, joy for evermore. In this hope I sleep quietly; and would sleep so, were it not the noise of the devil, and sin's feet, and the cries of an unbelieving heart awaken me; but for the present, I have nothing whereof I can accuse Christ's cross.—*Rutherford.*

THE BELIEVER'S DEATH.

THOUGH a believer may have his darkness, doubts, and fears, and many conflicts of soul, while on his dying bed, yet usually these are all over and gone, before his last moments come. From the gracious promises of God to be with his people even unto death; and from the Scriptural accounts of dying saints; and from the observations I have made through the course of my life, I am of opinion that generally the people of God die comfortably; their spiritual enemies being made to be as still as a stone, while they pass through Jordan.—*Gill.*

As a man that takes a walk in his garden, and spying a beautiful full-blown flower, crops it and puts it into his bosom, so the Lord takes his walks in his gardens, the churches, and gathers his lilies, souls fully ripe for glory, and with delight takes them to himself.—*Gill.*

PRAYER.—Sometimes, perhaps, thou hearest another Christian pray with much freedom and fluency while thou canst hardly get out a few broken words.   Hence, thou art ready to accuse thyself and to admire him ; as if the gilding of the key made it open the door the better.—*Gurnall.*

NAOMI—THE WIDOW COMFORTED.

THE book of Ruth is a delightful narrative. Its charming simplicity, its interesting allusions to the customs of a remote age, its delineations of character so fresh and lifelike, its sweet pathos, and the pure and lofty sentiments which it breathes, have ever made it a favorite with all readers of taste and feeling.   Many are the points of interest which it suggests, but our present purpose confines us to the evidence it furnishes that Jehovah is the widow's God.

This narrative shows that, through all the changes of Naomi's lot, even when the clouds lowered most darkly, she was never forsaken. Each successive trial only served to reveal more clearly the power and mercy of her fathers' God Let, then, the sorrowful widow, whose tearful eye may trace these pages, and she, especially, who in life's decline, treasures in her heart the mournful memory of one early loved but too early lost, derive strength and comfort from this record of God's faithfulness and compassion.

Naomi is now in a strange land, whither a famine in her own country had forced her family. It is a land of spiritual darkness, and she is far from the home of her childhood; but her husband is with her, and we may believe that, leaning upon him, she cheerfully endures the pains of exile. And they hope, perhaps, ere long to return to their beloved Judea.

But who can foresee the clouds that may darken the future? In their happy home the voice of anguish is at length heard. Naomi sits "beneath the shadow of a great affliction." She is a widow. Her staff is broken. The light of her dwelling is quenched. Who of her kindred shall weep with her? Who direct her to Abraham's God? She is sad and desolate. And yet Naomi is not alone. He who had promised to be the husband of the widow is with her. He sustained her, and opened new sources of support and happiness.

Time passes on, and her children, the thought of whose helplessness had, perhaps, deepened her grief, become the helpers of her joy. The silence of the inspired record, makes it proper to infer that, by their marriage with the daughters of the land, they were not enticed away from the God of their fathers, as she might have feared would be the case. The touching scene of her departure from the land of Moab, shows that a strong attachment existed between herself and her daughters-in-law. Their society and assistance contributed to her happiness. Thus was God fulfilling, in her experience, the promises he has made to his children.

But another and terrible trial awaits her. Her husband is no more, and now her sons follow him. Three widows are mourning beneath the same roof. Now does Naomi's cup of bitterness overflow. She can no longer stay in this valley of Achor; and though in going, she must leave the graves of her husband and sons, yet every object opens her wounds afresh, and she sighs for her native land, where her kindred dwell, and where the true God is worshipped. She hears, too, that "the Lord has visited his people in giving them bread." Sad indeed is her condition, but "as her day is, such is her strength." She summons up courage to return.

And now the three lonely widows are on their way to Bethlehem. Perceiving in the mind of at least one of her daughters-in-law, sadness at quitting her native land, Naomi, with a noble disinterestedness united with a degree of self-abandonment, such as deep affliction sometimes produces, urges their return. "It grieveth me much for your sakes," is her language, "that the hand of the Lord is gone out against me." In this she manifests a pious recognition of God's hand in her afflictions, attended with a sad feeling of desolation, which makes her almost careless of her own future lot. She would be willing to pursue her journey alone. The future is dark, and how can she be so selfish as to wish to sadden their younger hearts by uniting their fortunes with hers? "Affliction follows me like a shadow," she seems to say,—"then go, my daughters, where the sun may shine bright upon your path."

And yet she can but have trembled for the decision. Will they abandon me, a helpless stranger, to pursue my solitary way? This was a dark hour for Naomi. The clouds had been gathering around her, one by one, till she was enwrapped in the deepest gloom.

But the widow's God was with her, and he moved the heart of the gentle, affectionate, pious Ruth, to cleave to her mother-in-law. How beautiful then shone forth from out the gloom of those doubtful moments, the deep, pure, holy love, which made that daughter so ready to forsake sister, and people, and country, for the sake of Naomi and Naomi's God. And what a touching proof was this of the Almighty's gracious remembrance of the widow in her affliction. The light of love that here beamed forth so brightly upon poor Naomi's darkness, illumined all the rest of her pilgrimage. Then were these two hearts knit together by the strongest and holiest ties.

The two travellers have reached Bethlehem, and here Naomi's grief opens afresh. What thoughts rushed into her mind ?   Through these gates, and along these streets, and from out that house, had gone forth a whole family—companions in exile,—but she alone returns, a widow and childless !   And when the citizens of the place, deeply moved at her coming, said, " is this Naomi ?" she said to them, " Call me not Naomi, *pleasant*,—call me Mara, *bitter*,—for the Almighty hath dealt very bitterly with me.   I went out full, and the Lord hath brought me home again empty ; why, then, call ye me Naomi, seeing the Lord hath testified against me, and the Almighty hath afflicted me ?"

Does the Lord leave her to these melancholy thoughts ?   No.   Brighter days are before her. The two widows dwell in the city of Naomi's youth, and gather their humble living in accordance with the simple customs of the land, and the merciful provisions of Israel's God.   Here, among friends, the sadness that had so long rested upon her spirit was in a measure removed, and when Ruth returned one evening laden with the fruits of a very successful gleaning in the field of Boaz, and told her mother-in-law the name and kindness of their benefactor, Naomi's heart broke forth in gratitude and praise;—" Blessed be he of the Lord, who has not left off his kindness to the living and the dead."

And now the day of joy begins to break, and the shadows to flee away. From this hour may she, the long sorrow-stricken widow, date some of her happiest days. That benefactor in the harvest-field was a near kinsman, a man of wealth, and influence, and generous disposition, and God inclined his heart tenderly and warmly towards Ruth. There was, doubtless, a fascination, for such a man, in her simple, gentle, modest demeanor, and in her self-sacrificing affection for Naomi, which, with the sympathy he felt in the sorrows of both, made him her willing captive.

Soon, the humble gleaner in the harvest-field —the poor Moabitish stranger—becomes the honored and beloved wife of the rich, the noble Boaz; and beneath his roof, Naomi, who had wished to be called Mara for the bitterness of her grief finds her heart singing for joy. And when at length a son was born of Ruth, and " she took it, and laid it in-her own bosom, and became its nurse," she must have responded with all her heart to the kind and devout expressions of the women,—" Blessed be the Lord, who hath not left thee this day without a kinsman, that his name may be famous in Israel. And he shall be unto thee a restorer of thy life, and a nourisher of thine old age; for thy daughter-in-law, which loveth thee, who is better to thee than seven sons, hath borne him."

Here at last, after so many wanderings and trials, the good Naomi finds a peaceful home for the evening of her days. Now she can see·that God had always been mindful of her, even when her course was the most dark and crooked. Having sufficiently tried her in the furnace, he has brought her forth into a " wealthy place"— yea, her last days, which she had feared would be her saddest, are the most richly fraught with blessing.

And there was mercy towards her which she never knew on earth. Could she have looked through her tears forward to coming ages, and have seen that from the son fondled in her arms, and born of that daughter brought from Gentile Moab, was to spring the mighty David, and his greater son, the Messiah, she would have blessed God for all the windings of her pilgrimage, and have ever felt that in her afflictions even, not Mara, but Naomi, was her most fitting name.

Let the widow—solitary and aged—her husband gone—her children, it may be, resting by his side, confirm her faith and hope by Naomi's history. Let her catch in this an insight into the mysteries of providence. Let her learn to " trust where she cannot trace," and remember that what she knows not now of God's designs in her afflictions, she shall know hereafter if she be his child, and that what to her short, dim vision may seem cause only for sorrow and distrust, may be intimately connected, in the plan of infinite wisdom, with purposes of mercy to herself and others. God's purposes ripen every hour, not only when the sun of prosperity is shining, but when the rains descend, and the winds blow, and the heart fails through fear. Paradise shall unfold them in glorious perfection.

LIVE BY THE DAY.

I AM at present, through mercy, in perfect health, but it becomes me to live with the Lord *by the day*, and to carry my life in my hand, leaving to-morrow with the Lord. At all times we are little aware what the next day may bring forth, but at my advanced age everything is more and more precarious from day to day. I am in continual expectation of being either called away or laid aside. I may perhaps still live some years, and the Lord is so gracious to me in all my concerns, that none can have less reason to be weary of living, excepting for the body of indwelling sin. My part is only to wait, and to pray that I may at last be found ready. The *how, when,* and *where* belong to him. Yes, the Lord pours contempt upon our proud boastings. —*John Newton, (Aged Pilgrim's Triumph.)*

CHRIST AN ALMIGHTY SAVIOUR.

I HAVE been enabled to commit my soul to him who says, " him that cometh I will in *no wise* cast out," and " who is able to save to the *uttermost.*" These two texts have been as two sheet-anchors, by which my soul has rode out many a storm, when otherwise hope would have failed. " In no wise " takes in all characters, and " to the uttermost " goes many a league beyond all difficulties. I recommend these anchors; they are sure and steadfast.—*John Newton, in his seven tieth year. (Aged Pilgrim's Triumph.)*

DEPENDANCE ON CHRIST.

New washing, renewed application of purchased redemption, by that sacred blood that sealeth the free covenant, is a thing of daily and hourly use to a poor sinner. Jesus who cleanseth and cureth the soul must be our song on this side of heaven's gates; and even when we have won the castle, then must we eternally sing, " Worthy is the Lamb who hath saved us and washed us in his own blood."—*Rutherford.*

SKETCH OF MRS. B. OF B.

A poet has beautifully asked, " Hath not life an Indian summer?" and well may we answer in the affirmative, when we see an aged disciple of Christ, who, having patiently suffered with him, is now waiting in cheerful trust to be glorified with him. As the rays of the morning sun illuminate our earth before his rising, so the bliss which awaits such a Christian in his Father's house on high, casts forward its rays to allure him upwards, and to show what that glory must be, whose faintest glimmerings amid pain and sorrow, shed such a halo around him.

Mrs. B. was a beautiful example of that class of Christians who enjoy in their last days a fore-taste of eternal glory. Her lot in life had ever been a humble one. Peace and plenty had crowned her youth and middle life; and even down to grey hairs, when friend and acquaint-ance, husband and many children, had been taken from her, there still were left an affectionate son and daughter to comfort her and to provide for her wants. But when past fourscore years, it pleased God in a sudden and painful manner to remove both from her sight. She was left alone—childless and a widow, with scanty means of support. The faithful, pious daughter, upon whose arm she had leaned, was first taken Aside from the loss itself, the circumstances of the bereavement were peculiarly trying. For months had the mother been deprived of her society and aid, while she, the tempted and suffering one, was confined in a lunatic asylum. And there did she die, away from her home. Then that aged mother turned to her son, her only surviving child. He was poor and burdened with a large family, but he was her son, and if he could not supply *all* her wants, he could sympa thize with her. But in a few days, while he was absent from home, she received word that he had suddenly sickened and died among strangers, and that she was left with his widow and six help ess little ones to look to God for bread.

It was under these circumstances that I accompanied her pastor to her dwelling. We ascended softly the narrow winding stairs, and knocked at the unpainted door. Tears were in my eyes: I had no word to say to one passing through such deep waters, and had only come to " weep with her." A cheerful voice answered our knocking, and we entered, but not to witness a picture of sorrow. The aged pilgrim rose, and with the aid of her staff came forward to meet us. Looking over her spectacles to recognise me, she soon saw that I was a stranger. On being told the name of her new visitor, she gave a cordial greeting, then looking out anxiously on the deep snow, she said, " You surely did not *walk?*" When told that we did, she seemed overcome with gratitude, and thanked us again and again for thinking of her.

The faded gown, which doubtless her own hands had woven in the days of her strength, the broad frilled cap of the coarsest cloth, the bowed form and the deeply furrowed face, the pleasant smile which seemed to have no right there (because I, in my ignorance, imagined that where there was affliction there must be deep gloom), all these made upon my mind an impression which can never be effaced.

She conversed freely and cheerfully with her pastor; she spoke of Christ; how merciful he was, and how increasingly precious to her soul. She mentioned the children of God, spoke of their love to one another, and particularly of their tenderness to herself, a poor unworthy one among them. She repeated the names of all who had called upon her in her affliction, and said that her stock of food was replenished before the last was gone, and that her fire had never been suffered to go out for want of fuel. "And now," she said, "I will let you see a letter I have received, which will show that the tender mercies of God are still around me." She rose, and leaning with one hand on her staff, reached a letter from a shelf above her, which she placed in her pastor's hand, with a request that he would read it aloud. Blessed pilgrim! every reading of that short epistle by friends who called to visit her, was to her a fresh confirmation of the truth of the rich promises on which she had so long relied. It was only a line from the superinten-dent of the insane hospital where her daughter had died; but it contained what to her pious heart was more than all the riches of earth, a statement that the afflicted one had become fully rational before her death, and had left earth with most triumphant joy.

The aged saint listened with a smile till the reading was finished, and then said, "When I first heard of my daughter's death, it was late in the afternoon. I had been eagerly waiting to hear that she was restored to her reason, and could again take care of her poor feeble mother. I had no word to say; I knew it was all right; and, although I did not then know any of the circumstances which now afford me so much comfort, I did leave her in His hands who does all things well. Still, it was a great stroke, and I thought I should not be able to sleep all night for thoughts of her. But I was mistaken: I went to bed early, as is my custom, and soon fell into a quiet sleep, which was not broken till the sun awoke me, shining in my face. This had not happened before for years, as my infirmities often keep me awake for hours. " It is so," she said, smiling; " 'he giveth his beloved sleep.' When I did awake, my heart was full of praise to God for all his mercies to me. Since this letter came, and I find that my prayers have been answered for my child, my heart is full, and when I cannot sleep, he giveth me ' songs in the night.' Sometimes I get impatient to be gone, and, as I can do nothing for God, and am only a trouble to others, I wonder why I am kept here." Her pastor reminded her that our Heavenly Father, after having accomplished the great work of conforming the will of a Christian to his own will, may keep him still on earth for an example to others, that weaker Christians, as well as those who know not God, may see the power of his grace. He said he believed that she was still among the living, in order that her placid and even cheerful temper amid severe and repeated afflictions, might glorify God. " I never thought of that before," she said, while a smile which cannot be described, lighted up her face. "I will try to be patient till his time comes." Thus she talked of heaven and of going home, as we do upon everyday topics. And she did not wait, as some do, to change the countenance and tone of voice. Hers was the religion of love and cheerful submission, and prayer and praise were the natural breathings of her heart. When asked what was the principal evidence of her adoption, she reflected a moment, and then said with animation, "Oh, Jesus is *so* precious!" "But were you always as free from doubts and desponding fears as you now are?" "Oh! no, no," she quickly replied; "in the earlier part of my Christian life, whenever I sinned, I went a long time mourning and doubting, before I could feel an evidence of forgiveness; but now, when I have sinned, and I lose my joy, I look right to Christ. Then my peace is restored. I know more of Christ now than I did in those days."

There was in her room a want of many things necessary for the comfort of one so feeble, and feeling that it would be an honor to perform the humblest service for one so like my blessed Master, I invited her to spend a few days at my house.   I thought I might, by proper care, lessen her sufferings, and in the meantime cleanse the dingy walls of her chamber, and add some articles of comfort to her little home.   She gratefully but modestly declined my invitation, and when I pressed her still further, promising her a fire in her sleeping room, and many other attentions, she seemed pained at my earnestness, and saw that she must assign a reason for not granting my request.   Putting on an expression peculiarly her own, she said, " When you expect company whom you have long been urging to come to your house, you never go out, do you ? Well, I am looking anxiously every night for my Master, and when he comes, I wish him to find me at home watching !"   Her reason was satisfactory, and I ceased striving to allure her from the humble abode made sacred by the frequent visits of Him whom her soul loved.

Blessed woman !   She watched for his coming, as those who watch for the morning ; nor were her vigils long kept in vain.   Those faded eyes shall watch no more, having long ago seen the King in his beauty.   That longing heart shall pant no more for holiness, for she is **now** satisfied, having awaked in His likeness. How glorious for her the change! The hoary head, which here pressed the humble pillow through long nights of weariness and pain, wears now the starry crown of the redeemed in the land where there is no more night; the faltering limbs, which here almost refused to bear their burden, now stand in new strength upon Mount Zion, and walk the golden streets of the new Jerusalem; the palsied hand, which strove in vain to supply her few wants below, now strikes the chords of her golden harp to the praise of the Lamb. She is gone from among those who felt it a high privilege to give her even a cup of water in the name of Christ, but her memory is still fragrant among them, and it is hoped that this imperfect sketch of one who was honored with special grace, may invite others to strive after that close communion with heaven, which rendered a humble child of God so conspicuous for piety, and which enabled her to "bear fruit in old age."—*J. D. C.*

EMBLEM OF A DEPARTING SAINT.

A CLOUD lay cradled near the setting sun,
  A gleam of crimson tinged its braided snow;

5*

Long had I watched the glory moving on
 O'er the still radiance of the lake below :
Tranquil its spirit seemed, and floated slow,
 E'en in its very motion there was rest,
While every breath of eve that chanced to blow
 Wafted the traveller to the beauteous west.
Emblem, methought, of the departed soul,
 To whose white robe the gleam of bliss is given,
And by the breath of mercy made to roll
 Right onward to the golden gates of heaven ;
Where to the eye of faith it peaceful lies,
 And tells to man his glorious destinies.

Songs for the Sabbath.

THE DEATH OF BELIEVERS.

CHRISTIAN believers die " in the Lord." They
are now in him as the branch is in the vine ;
and he is now in them by his Holy Spirit.   To
this he alludes in the following passage : " He that
abideth in me, and I in him, the same bringeth
forth much fruit."   The union of the soul and
body is dissolved by death ; but the union of the
soul to Christ remains unbroken in that solemn
hour.   Then the believer cleaves to him with
purpose of heart ; and he cleaves to the believer in
mercy and love.   This sacred union with Jesus,
when the soul is departing hence, is the greatest

blessing that can be enjoyed in that awful hour. It secures to the believer the support of the almighty Saviour; it fills his soul with holy joy; it strengthens his hope; it brightens his prospects; it gives him the victory. Such a death is truly happy; and is more to be desired than all the wealth and power of this world of shadows.—*Edmondson.*

Dr. Payson, when racked with pain and near to death, exclaimed, " Oh, what a blessed thing it is to lose one's will! Since I have lost my will, I have found happiness. There can be no such thing as disappointment to me, for I have no desire, but that God's will may be accomplished."

"LET ME GO, FOR THE DAY BREAKETH."

<blockquote>
Let me go, the day is breaking,
  Earthly scenes ar[illegible]
Joys that were m[illegible]g,
  Hopes and fear[illegible] the past.
Earthly visions now are darkling,
  And the city's golden glow
Gleams before me, pure and sparkling,
  In the distance—let me go!
</blockquote>

Angel hosts, resplendent shining,
    Wait me at the river's side,
And my eager heart is pining
    But to meet them on the tide.
I can see the life-founts gushing,
    I can hear their silvery flow ;
Joys, a countless throng, are rushing
    On my spirit—let me go !

He, the wounded, the forsaken,
    In the death-hour sore dismayed,
All my grief and fear has taken,
    All my debt of sin has paid.
I can see his God-like brightness,
    Through the form he wore below,
On a throne of dazzling whiteness,
    And he calls me—let me go.

Friends, the early loved, the cherished,
    Parted from our paths like dew,
With the mortal have not perished—
    I behold them pure and true ;
Lovelier i[illegible]minion,
    E'en th[illegible]ed them so :
And they sta[illegible]oping pinion
    To enfold me—[illegible] go !

Lay me gently on my pillow,
    Weary are my thorn-pierced feet ;

Christ has calmed that boisterous pillow,
  And the rest beyond is sweet.
Could ye share the glorious vision,
  Ye would not detain me so ;
Now the homeward gales Elysian
  Woo my spirit—let me go !

Central Christian Herald.

THE BIBLE.—The new convert, dazzled over its pages with the ecstasy of his new-found hope, yet cannot as deeply and ardently love it, as he will do when a grey-headed patriarch, years after, he turns afresh its wondrous leaves, to adore the ever-full freshness of its lessons, and to remember all the lights it has cast upon his weary pathway.—*W. R. Williams.*

THERE are *silver* books, and a very few *golden* books : but I have one worth more than all, called the Bible ; and that is a book of *bank-notes.—Newton.*

TRUST IN GOD.

WITH the Patriarch's joy
Thy call I follow to the land unknown ;
I trust in thee, and know in whom I trust :
Or life or death, is equal : neither weighs ;
All weight in this—oh, let me live to thee !—*Young.*

THE CHRISTIAN'S PROSPECT.

THE best prospect, when faith is in exercise, is before us, especially to those who are far advanced in years. I am now old, and I know not the day of my death; and can it be that I am within a few years, perhaps months, or weeks, of joining in the songs and sharing in the joys of those who are now before the throne? that I may expect soon to see my Saviour without a veil, face to face, in all his glory, and in all his love? If so, why am I thus? Why am I no more affected and enlivened by this blessed hope, which, finally, as it impresses me, I would not part with for a thousand worlds! Alas! a body of sin and unbelief weighs me down. So, when a bird with a stone tied to its foot attempts to fly, the weight pulls it back, and it flutters its wings in vain. Our life is safely hid with Christ in God, but it will be a life of warfare while we continue here; let us fight on: the Captain of our salvation is near. See! he holds the prize in view! Hark! he speaks, and says, " Be thou faithful unto death, and I will give thee a crown of life!"—*John Newton.* (*Aged Pilgrim's Triumph.*)

The Believer awaiting the Coming of Christ.—Persuade yourself the King is coming. Read his letter sent before him, " Behold, I come quickly :" Wait with the wearied night-watch, for the breaking of the eastern sky, and think that ye have not a morrow ; as the wise father said, who being invited against to-morrow to dine with his friends, answered, " Those many days I had no morrow at all."—*Rutherford.*

THE LOVE OF CHRIST IN THE SUFFERINGS OF HIS DISCIPLES.

In whatever aspect we view it, the love of Christ is marvellous. The word of God affirms that it passeth knowledge, and no Christian has ever fathomed it. When we contemplate it as moving the Saviour to visit the earth, and die upon the cross for his enemies, we are led to exclaim, Was there ever love like this?

But, perhaps, the course of discipline to which the Redeemer subjects his disciples, in maturing them for heaven, affords, in some respects, the most touching proof of his love. In order to effect their complete purification, they need to be cast into the furnace, to feel the flames of affliction kindling about them. This is a painful, often an excruciating process, especially as it tends to awaken the latent iniquity of the heart, and occasions inward conflicts between nature and grace, the most violent and distressing In the midst of the fires the disciple cries out, " My sufferings are greater than I can bear !" or, perhaps, " My hope is gone !"

Where, now, is the Saviour during these painful experiences, extended, it may be, through long years?   Is it thus he manifests his love to his chosen ones, or has he forgotten to be gracious ? Why does he not quench these flames ? Why not heed these mournful cries ? Love is the answer ; yes, love more than human ; love so pure and strong, as to silence for the time the suggestions of mere sympathy ; love that longs to behold its own bright and beauteous image in the person of a disciple, and that can stand by and bear to see that beloved, ransomed one enduring more than tongue can express, while the dross is vanishing in the furnace. Yes, tried and fearful soul, your Saviour is ever near you, he looks upon you, he loves you, he is touched with the feeling of your infirmity, he sympathizes with every groan you utter, for you are a member of his own body, and he well remembers the anguish of his own heart when on earth; but his love looks beyond the present moment to future years, to the hour of death, to heaven, and resolves to do for you what shall inconceivably augment your holiness and your bliss eternally. His love kindles the fire, and keeps it burning, but when the dross shall be consumed, and your spirit meek and quiet "like a weaned child," oh, with what double rapture will he draw you from the furnace, fold you in his arms, and smile upon you with a look that will reveal something of heaven! And as you review all the trials you have endured, you will say, It was all of love. Yes, the time will come when you will regard every stroke as given in mercy, and bless God that there was not one less. Human love is not equal to this. It is blind and feeble. It is sometimes untrue, by reason of its frailty. But Christ's love never faileth. It infinitely transcends all human infirmity. It can bear to be considered for a time coldness and desertion, for it looks to the believer's ultimate and exceeding greater good, and well knows that the future will reveal its true intent and heavenly purity.

THE godly sow in tears and reap in joy. The seed-time is commonly waterish and lowering. I will be content with a wet spring, so I may be sure of a clear and joyful harvest.—*Bishop Hall.*

THE TWO WONDERS.—"Two things," says Pearce, " are matter of daily astonishment to me —the *readiness* of Christ to come from heaven to. earth for me; and my *backwardness* to rise from earth to heaven for him."

TO AN AFFLICTED LADY.

WHEN ye are come to the other side of the water, and have set down your foot on the shore of glorious eternity, and look back again to the waters, and to your wearisome journey, and shall see in that clear glass of endless glory, nearer to the bottom of God's wisdom, you shall then be forced to say : If God had done otherwise with me than he hath done, I had never come to the enjoying of this crown of glory. It is your part now to believe, and suffer, and hope, and wait on; for I protest in the presence of that all-discerning eye, who knoweth what I write, and what I think that I would not want the sweet experience of the consolations of God, for all the bitterness of affliction; nay, whether God come to his children with a rod or a crown, if he come himself with it, it is well; welcome, welcome, Jesus, what may soever then come, if we can get a sight of thee. And sure I am, it is better to be sick, providing Christ come to the bed-side and draw the curtains, and say, "Courage, I am thy salvation," than to enjoy health, and never to be visited of God.—*Rutherford.*

It is enough that the Lord hath promised you great things; only let the time of bestowing them be in his own carving. It is not for us to set an hour-glass to the Creator of time.—*Rutherford.*

THOUGHTS OF HEAVEN.

I am a stranger here below, my home is above. Yet I can think too well of these foreign vanities, and cannot think enough of my home. Surely that is not so far above my head as my thoughts; neither doth so far pass me in distance as in comprehension ; and yet I would not stand so much upon conceiving, if I could admire it enough : but my strait heart is filled with a little wonder, and hath no room for the greatest part of glory that remaineth. O God, what happiness hast thou prepared for thy chosen ! What a purchase was this, worthy of the blood of such a Saviour ! As yet I do but look towards it afar off, but it is easy to see by the outside how goodly it is within ; although, as thine house on earth, so that above, hath more glory within than can be bewrayed by the outer appearance. The outer part of thy tabernacle here below is but an earthly and base substance, but within it is furnished with a living, spiritual, and heavenly guest ; so the outer heavens, though they be as gold to all other material creatures, yet they are but dross to thee ! Yet how are even the outmost walls of that house of thine beautified with glorious lights, whereof every one is a world for bigness and as a heaven for goodliness ! O teach me by this to long after and wonder at the inner part, before thou lettest me come in to behold it ! *—Bishop Hall.*

LOOKING HEAVENWARD.

THE golden palace of my God
   Towering above the clouds I see :
Beyond the cherubs' bright abode,
. Higher than angels' thoughts can be.
How can I in these courts appear
   Without a wedding-garment on ?
Conduct me, thou Life-giver, there,
   Conduct me to thy glorious throne !
And clothe me with thy robes of light,
   And lead me through sin's darksome night,
My Saviour and my God !

THE righteous shall flourish like the palm-tree: he shall grow like a cedar in Lebanon. Those that be planted in the house of the Lord shall flourish in the courts of our God. They shall still bring forth fruit in old age ; they shall be fat and flourishing, to show that the Lord is upright: he is my rock, and there is no unrighteousness in him.—*Psalm* xcii. 12–15.

DEATH is the friend of grace and the enemy of nature.—*Dodd.*

INFANCY, YOUTH, AND AGE.

Our infancy is full of folly ; youth, of disorder and toil; age, of infirmity. Each time hath his burden, and that which may justly work our weariness. Yet infancy longeth after youth, and youth after more age, and he that is very old, as he is a child for simplicity, so he would be for years. I account old age the best of three ; partly, for that it hath passed through the folly and disorder of the others ; partly, for that the inconveniences of this are but bodily, with a bettered estate of the mind ; and partly, for that it is nearest to dissolution. There is nothing more miserable than an old man that would be young again. It was an answer worthy the commendations of Petrarch, who, when his friend bemoaned his age appearing in his white temples, telling him he was sorry to see him look so old, replied, " Nay, be sorry rather that I was ever young, to be a fool."—*Bishop Hall.*

DAYS GONE BY.

Though we charge to-day with fleetness,
  Though we dread to-morrow's sky,
There's a melancholy sweetness
  In the name of days gone by.

Yes, though Time has laid his finger
  On them, still with streaming eye
There are spots where I can linger,
  Sacred to the days gone by.

Oft as memory's glance is ranging
  Over scenes that cannot die,
Then I feel that all is changing,
  Then I weep the days gone by.

Sorrowful should I be, and lonely,
  Were not all the same as I,
'Tis for all, not my lot only,
  To lament the days gone by.

Cease, fond heart,—to thee are given
  Hopes of better things on high,
There is still a coming heaven,
  Brighter than the days gone by.

Faith lifts off the sable curtain,
  Hiding huge eternity ;
Hope accounts her prize as certain,
  And forgets the days gone by.

Love in grateful adoration
  Bids distrust and sorrow fly,
And with glad anticipation
  Calms regret for days gone by.—*Tupper.*

THE HAPPINESS OF THE CHRISTIAN.

THERE is no man so happy as the Christian. When he looks up into heaven, he thinks, " That is my home; the God that made it and owns it is my Father; the angels, more glorious in nature than myself, are my attendants; mine enemies are my vassals." Yea, those things which are the terriblest of all to the wicked, are most pleasant to him. When he hears God thunder above his head, he thinks, " This is the voice of my Father." When he remembereth the tribunal of the last judgment, he thinks, " It is my Saviour that sits in it." When death comes, he esteems it but as the angel set before paradise, which with one blow admits him to eternal joy. And, which is most of all, nothing in earth or hell can make him miserable. There is nothing in the world worth envying but the Christian.—*Bishop Hall.*

LESSON OF CONTENTMENT.

* * * LOOK in on Bunyan in the dungeon. It is, perhaps, an hour of solitude and sadness. He sees through the grating the quivering leaf

and the green hedge. They are free to breathe
the unfettered air, and to bask beneath the open
sky. He is shut up. He sees the herds roaming
at their will unconfined, and hears the call of the
bird as it soars and sings, and sees perhaps some
godless sportsman whom he knows amongst his
scorners and persecutors, merry and unquestioned
on his way afield. Equipages roll past. Rank,
and beauty, and wealth, and learning, adorn their
tenants. Does he envy the quivering leaf, and
the air-swept hedge, and the uncaged lark, or
begrudge the hunter his sports, or the rich, and
gay, and wise, their enjoyment of life ? They
have the goods of earth. Some have vegetable
life, and the others animal life, and the others
intellectual life, but he has *spiritual* life. In his
dungeon he is the Lord's freeman. In his
oppression, and penury; and lowly ignorance, he
is visited, and taught, and comforted of God.
And in that lonely prisoner, tagging his laces, or
thumbing the martyr's sad, glad story, or bowed
over his Bible, you have seen the happiest,
greatest, wisest, and safest man of them all.—*W
R. Williams.*

6

THE DESERTED HOMESTEAD.

Gloom is upon thy lonely hearth,
O silent house! once filled with mirth;
Sorrow is in the breezy sound
Of thy tall poplars whispering. round.

The shadow of departed hours
Hangs dim upon thine early flowers;
E'en in thy sunshine seems to brood
Something more deep than solitude.

Fair art thou, fair to strangers' gaze,
Mine own sweet home of other days!
My children's birth-place! yet for me
It is too much to look on thee!

Too much, for all about thee spread,
I feel the memory of the dead,
And almost linger for the feet
That never more my step shall meet.

The looks, the smiles, all vanished now,
Follow me where thy roses blow;
The echoes of kind household words
Are with me midst thy singing birds.

Till my heart dies, it dies away
In yearnings, for what might not stay;
For love which ne'er deceived thy trust,
For all which went with "dust to dust."

What now is left me but to raise
From thee, lone spot! my spirit's gaze,
To lift, through tears, my straining eye
Up to my Father's house on high?

Oh, many are the mansions there,
But not in one hath grief a share!
No haunting shades from things gone by
May there o'ersweep the unchanging sky.

And they are there, whose long-loved mien
In earthly home no more is seen;
Whose places where they smiling sate,
Are left unto us desolate.

We miss them when the board is spread,
We miss them when the prayer is said,
Upon our dreams their dying eyes
In still and mournful fondness rise.

But they are where these longings vain
Trouble no more the heart and brain;
The sadness of this aching love
Dims not our Father's house above.

Ye are at rest, and I in tears,
Ye dwellers of immortal spheres!
Under the poplar boughs I stand,
And mourn the broken household band.

But by your life of lowly faith,
And by your joyful hope in death,

Guide me, till on some brighter shore
The severed wreath is bound once more.

Holy ye were, and good, and true!
No change can cloud my thoughts of you;
Guide me like you to live and die,
And reach my Father's house on high!—*Hemans.*

THE AGED SAINT A WITNESS FOR GOD.

The Christian laden with years and infirmity often wonders why he is permitted to outlive, as he thinks, his usefulness. As he sits in his lonely chamber, he asks himself with sadness, "What good am I doing? for what purpose am I spared?"

Aged disciple, be assured that your heavenly Father must have some wise design in your continuing to live, or you would not be alive. It is he that prolongs your days, and he does nothing in vain.

But we may easily perceive important respects in which a child of God can exert a happy influence, even in extreme old age.

He is a powerful witness for *the truth and value of religion.* The unbeliever may scornfully point to the young convert rejoicing in the glow of his early love, and say, In a few months this ardent love will cool into indifference or positive disregard,—religion is a mere transient impulse. In reply, we will bid him look to that aged pilgrim who, with advancing years, clings to the religion of Christ with a firmer and more confiding grasp, and an ever growing conviction of its truth; and who, when perhaps the trace of all else has been effaced from the mind, still remembers Christ, and weeps at the very mention of his name. Yes, that poor widow, in her humble cottage, bowed beneath a load of years, but trustful, and joyfully longing for her change to come, is a mighty witness for God. Her quiet influence is powerful through all the circle of her acquaintance. It silences the sceptic, it confirms the faith of the doubting.

And when to length of years, we add the trials, disappointments, and bereavements, which in long and perhaps quick succession have been the pilgrim's lot, and find that amid them all, his confidence in God has remained unshaken, his love to the Saviour unabated, and that the "hope" which had dawned upon the spring-time of his life, shines still undimmed in old age, growing brighter unto the perfect day, we may well!

believe that a religion which bears such fruit is indeed divine.

Besides the testimony to the truth and value of religion by so long a continuance in the faith of Christ, there may be the present daily witness of a patient submission to the will of God under pains and infirmities. The saint may glorify God, not only by *doing*, but by *suffering* his will; by standing still, or lying passive in his hands; by being willing to be set aside from those active labors which had long been his delight, and to *be* and to *do* nothing, if God so ordain; by calmly, meekly waiting his will, whether to live or die. These are the most difficult and sublime achievements of faith; and these are often the blessed fruits of pious old age.

Was it in vain that John Newton and Rowland Hill passed the limit of fourscore years, when their old age exhibited such a heavenly piety, breathed forth such a spirit of trust in God? Aged saint, be patient, submissive, cheerful, and you live not in vain.

What *maturity of experience* can the aged pilgrim bring to the edification and comfort of the saints? He may be no longer a soldier in active service, but as a veteran retired from the field, covered perhaps with honorable scars, he can recount his spiritual conflicts, how he feared defeat and found relief, and how worthy and mighty is the Captain of salvation. As a way-worn pilgrim, he can tell of the City of Destruction, of the Slough of Despond, of the terrible Mount Sinai, of Bye-Path Meadow, of Doubting Castle, of the fierce Apollyon, of the Valley of Humiliation, and the Valley of the Shadow of Death; and he can also tell of the good Evangelist, of the blessed Cross, of the House of the Interpreter, and the House Beautiful, of the Sword of the Spirit, of the Delectable Mountain, and the Land Beulah.

Aged pilgrim, you can talk, as the younger cannot, of the faithfulness of a covenant God in answering prayer, fulfilling promises, delivering from temptation and danger. You can say, "I have been young and now am old; yet have I not seen the righteous forsaken, nor his seed begging bread." Your tremulous voice can sing in strains such as the young Christian cannot reach, of the preciousness of the Redeemer, of his tenderness and long-suffering, of the infinite freeness and fulness of his redemption, and of the power of his blessed intercession. You can speak of victories where he can mention little more than conflicts; and you can tell him how he too may triumph through grace. You can best explain the secret of peace and joy in Christ, for your experience has taught you to pass beyond and above your sins and your doings, at once and unreservedly to him.

Blessed be God, that he permits his churches to possess such witnesses for the truth and excellence of the gospel,—such guides to the inexperienced. With firmer and more joyful steps' we run the race set before us, cheered onward by such a cloud of witnesses who are ahead of us in the course, and who have almost attained the goal and the crown.

And there is one weapon which even the palsied arm of age may wield, the weapon of *prayer*. In the use of this, to which he has been so long accustomed, the aged saint may do much for the cause of God. If his frail body cannot reach the sanctuary, his devout spirit may soar to the Throne, and bring thence to earth the choicest blessings. With his fervent petitions, heard by no ear but God's, uttered perhaps in the silence of night, eternity may show that the most glorious results were connected.

Therefore, aged pilgrim, while you live, pray, for while you pray you live. Your season of usefulness is not ended. God, your Father, loves you, and for the sake of his dear Son he will not suffer one of your pious thoughts or aspirations to fall to the ground. He will treasure them up, and in the great day when his jewels are gathered in, an assembled universe shall know every sigh you breathed in secret for the cause of Christ; and it shall receive a large reward through grace. You live, therefore, because your work on earth is not yet done. That ended, and you shall be released.

TESTIMONY OF AN AGED CHRISTIAN
(NEAR THE 60TH YEAR OF HER AGE).

I LEAVE it as my testimony that God has been a father to the fatherless, a husband to the widow, the stranger's shield, and orphan's stay. Even to hoar years and old age he has carried me, and *not one good word has failed* of all that he has promised. 'He has done all things well,' and at this day I am richer and happier than ever I was in my life. Not that I am yet made free from sin; that is still my burden;—want of love and gratitude, indolence in commanded duty, self-will and nestling in the creature. But my heart's wish and earnest desire is conformity. The bent of my will is for God; and if my heart deceive me not, my God is the centre of my best affections. This God is my God. He will guide me even unto death, through death, and be my portion through eternity. —*Isabella Graham.*

THE AGED AND EXPERIENCED CHRISTIAN.— There is not a nobler sight in the world than the aged and experienced Christian, who, having been sifted in the sieve of temptation, stands forth as a confirmer of the assaulted,—testifying from his own trials the reality of religion; and meeting by his warnings, and directions, and consolations, the cases of all those who may be tempted to doubt.—*Cecil.*

OLD AGE.

The scathed and leafless tree may seem
  Old age's mournful sign,
Yet on its bark may sunshine gleam,
  And moonlight softly shine.

Thus on the cheek of age, shall rest
  The light of days gone by,
Calm as the glories of the west,
  When night is drawing nigh.

As round the scathed trunk fondly clings
  The ivy, green and strong,
Repaying, by the grace it brings,
  The succor granted long ;

So round benevolent old age
  May objects yet survive,
Whose greenness can the heart engage,
  And keep the soul alive.—*Burton.*

THE CROSS OF CHRIST.—The light of the sun is always the same, but it shines brightest to us at noon ; the Cross of Christ was the noontide of everlasting love—the meridian splendor of eternal mercy.—*M'Laurin.*

THE BEAUTY OF HOLINESS.

HOLINESS, wherever seen, has its own heaven-.y beauty, outshining all the glory of the world In man it is the reflection of God's own excellence, for he is "glorious in holiness." Its light is kindled at the Throne. It is that which adorns the angels and makes heaven glorious. And to whatever has a grace of its own, this imparts new lustre, or if aught have in itself no attraction, this can hide its deformity and make it beautiful. There is a charm in intellectual power, but, by high pre-eminence,

> How beautiful is genius when combined
> With holiness.

There is an unseemliness in mental dulness and ignorance, which awakens pity or contempt; yet even here, holiness may so brightly shine, the graces of the Spirit be so conspicuous, that we cannot but look on with admiration and wonder. And how soon, we think, will that stupid intellect sweep through the realm of truth and light with a seraph's power, and outstrip, it may be, many that now soar far beyond it.

But, though holiness have such intrinsic beauty, and confer such glory on all who possess it, so that they become "sons of God," being " partakers of his holiness," yet it awakens different kinds and degrees of interest, according to the aspects under which we view it.

Piety in very early childhood, refining the soul

from natural defilement, unfolds a soft pleasing grace, as if a flower of Paradise were opening here below its first unstained beauty, to show what human nature would have been, had not sin debased it.

Piety exhibits another beauty, as the Spirit lays his hand of gentle violence upon the youthful heart, taming its wild bounding passions which loved to roam at large in quest of pleasure, and lifting it upwards in calm contemplation to heaven.

When religion sanctifies manhood, it developes yet another beauty. Then it is seen in its manly proportions, revealing the beauty of strength and symmetry, of noble devotion to the cause of God amid difficulty and self-denial.

But, in some of its aspects, holiness assumes its loveliest charms, when associated with old age. It is then seen, not indeed in the fair spring of its early promise, or in the summer of its brightest sunshine, but in the autumn of its ripe, clustering vintage. It sheds around the soft mellow light of evening, when the bustle and glare of day are over. It does not so much excite our wonder, as win our love. It presents a quiet beauty—a picture of calm heavenly peace. Outward beauty perhaps is faded, the eye is dim, the voice unmusical, the forehead deeply furrowed with the traces of care and toil, the form bent beneath the burden of years, the step feeble and uncertain, and the countenance bereft of its once beaming expressiveness. But love has its seat there, and faith and hope, ornaments of grace, shining now in their own native lustre, borrowing little from adventitious charms. The aged saint often exhibits in richest perfection those quiet graces, which, though less showy, are more difficult of attainment, of finer quality, and more heavenly maturity, than those active endowments in which grace is often largely blended with and obscured by nature, and which therefore more attract the admiration of the world. It demands an " eye for the beautiful " in grace, an eye of spiritual discernment, to love holiness for its own sake, and when associated with natural infirmities or deformities. Holiness in old age displays itself not in a bold energy of thought and action, not in deeds of pious daring, but in a way yet more sublime, in a calm, patient, cheerful submission to God's will amid pain and infirmity ; in communion with him, and meditation upon his word; in believing his promises, and hoping unto the end. These are achievements, whose glory throws into the shade many of the deeds which the world applauds. The very feebleness and decaying beauty of age make holiness appear the more glorious, while we see it giving vigor to weakness, cheerfulness to grief, and hope to the certain prospect of death. *There* is the power of religion, the victory of faith. *There* is grace magnified, and God glorified. *There* we see the pilgrim, way-worn and weary, waiting at the threshold to hear the voice of his Father bidding him enter into rest. *There* is one almost redeemed from the corruptions of earth, and soon to wear a crown, and be a companion of angels. Behold his childlike faith. He lies down to sleep in the arms of his Saviour, hoping that the next light that breaks upon his vision may be that of eternity.

BARZILLAI.—And Barzillai came down from Rogelim, and went over Jordan with the king, to conduct him over Jordan. Now Barzillai was a very aged man, even fourscore years old: and he had provided the king of sustenance while he lay at Mahanaim: for he was a very great man. And the king said unto Barzillai, Come thou over with me, and I will feed thee with me in Jerusalem. And Barzillai said unto the king, How long have I to live, that I should go up with the king unto Jerusalem? I am this day fourscore years old: and can I discern between good and evil? can thy servant taste what I eat or what I drink? can I hear any more the voice of singing-men and singing-women? wherefore then should thy servant be yet a burden unto my lord the king! Thy servant will go a little way over Jordan with the king: and why should the king recompense it me with such a reward? Let thy servant, I pray thee, turn back again, that I may die in mine own city, and be buried by the grave of my father and my mother. But behold thy servant Chimham; let him go over with my lord the king; and do to him what shall seem good unto thee. . . . . And all the people went over Jordan. And when the king was come over, the king kissed Barzillai, and blessed him: and he returned unto his own place.—2 *Sam.* xix 31–39.

THE CYPRESS OF CEYLON.

[JOHN BATUTA, the celebrated Mussulman traveller of the fourteenth century, speaks of a cypress tree in Ceylon, universally held sacred by the natives, the leaves of which were said to fall only at certain intervals, and he who had the happiness to find and eat one of them, was restored at once to youth and vigor. The traveller saw several venerable Jogees or saints, sitting silent and motionless under the tree, patiently awaiting the falling of a leaf.]

THEY sat in silent watchfulness
  The sacred cypress tree about,
And, from beneath old wrinkled brows,
  Their failing eyes looked out.

Grey age and sickness waiting there,
  Through weary night and lingering day—
Grim as the idols at their side,
  And motionless as they.

Unheeded in the boughs above,
  The song of Ceylon's bird was sweet;
Unseen of them, the island flowers
  Bloomed brightly at their feet.

O'er them the tropic night-storm swept,
  The thunder crashed on rock and hill;
The cloud-fire in their eyeballs blazed,
  Yet there they waited still!

What was the world without to them ?
 The Moslem's sunset call—the dance
Of Ceylon maids—the passing gleam
 Of battle-flag and lance ?

They waited for that falling leaf,
 Of which the wondering Jogees sing ;
Which lends once more to wintry age
 The greenness of its spring.

Oh ! if these poor and blinded ones
 In trustful patience wait to feel,
O'er torpid pulse and failing limb,
 A youthful freshness steal ;

Shall we, who sit beneath that tree,
 Whose healing leaves of life are shed,
In answer to the breath of prayer,
 Upon the waiting head :

Not to restore our failing forms,
 And build the spirit's broken shrine,
But, on the fainting soul to shed
 A light and life divine :

Shall we grow weary in our watch,
 And murmur at the long delay !
Impatient of our Father's time,
 And his appointed way ?

Or, shall the stir of outward things
    Allure and claim the Christian's eye,
When on the heathen watcher's ear
    Their powerless murmurs die ?

Alas ! a deeper test of faith
    Than prison cell or martyr's stake,
The self-abasing watchfulness
    Of silent prayer may make.

Easier to smite with Peter's sword,
    Than " watch one hour" in humbling prayer :
Life's " great things," like the Syrian lord,
    Our hearts can do and dare.

But oh ! we shrink from Jordan's side,
    From waters which alone can save ;
And murmur for Abana's banks,
    And Pharpar's brighter wave.

Oh ! Thou, who in the garden's shade
    Didst wake the weary ones again,
Who slumbered at that fearful hour,
    Forgetful of thy pain :

Bend o'er us now, as over them,
    And set our sleep-bound spirits free,
Nor leave us slumbering in the watch
    Our souls should keep with Thee !—*J. G. Whittier*.

PEACE IN OLD AGE.

OLD AGE is commonly esteemed an evil, and we speak of its burdens in the language of pity, yet it has its own peculiar pleasures with which the younger stranger intermeddleth not. Within the aged heart, cold and dead as we sometimes deem it, may dwell a hidden life, whose calm twilight, though it seem dark in contrast with what we call the sunny days of childhood, is most truly peaceful and happy.

But such is not the case with all who have passed within the shadows of life's evening; and it is an interesting question, How may that evening be made to shine with a mild and cheerful radiance? If we interrogate the earth, its wide extent can send back no satisfactory answer. Its wealth may avert the anxieties and pains of poverty—that evil, great indeed when life is waning; its affectionate smiles and sympathies may render home a sanctuary of love; philosophy and refined social converse may perform their graceful ministry; and sometimes a peculiarly happy constitution may help the aged heart to sing amid trials and infirmities; but not all these combined, and existing in their best estate, can plant and nourish within the bosom of age true and substantial peace Under the most favorable circumstances of earthly bliss in which we can imagine the aged to be placed, thoughts and emotions must arise of a sombre hue, borrowing their dark shades from the past and future. From the past how many memories come thronging into the soul, of scenes and friends once dear but for ever gone, of hopes cherished only to be blighted, and of errors, mistakes, and sins, darkly tracing the whole course of life. And the "coming events" of life's close, and of the world beyond, so near at hand, must "cast their" deep "shadows before," and invest the future with gloom.

What now can displace from "the chambers of imagery" these gloomy visitants, that, in their stead, PEACE, that daughter of the skies may enter and diffuse her mild cheerfulness?

From all other responses let us turn, while we listen to the benignant voice of Jesus: "Peace I leave with you, my peace I give unto you; not as the world giveth give I unto you. Let not your heart be troubled, neither let it be afraid.

This is the only voice, whose sweet and powerful tones can hush into stillness the storm of passion and calm every anxious fear. It promises rest to the wayworn pilgrim: "Come unto me all ye that labor and are heavy laden, and I will give you rest. Take my yoke upon you, and learn of me; fo: I am meek and lowly in heart; and ye shall fi d rest unto your souls."

A livin, faith in the Son of God, as the Redeemer an d Advocate, brings this peace and rest, which fo m the truest solace of old age. With trust in Christ is connected the happy consciousness of s ns forgiven, of a heart purified, of adoption into God's family, and of heirship to heaven. With th s are connected also filial trust in God, meek submission to his will, and a comforting belief that all things are working together for good. This opens the way for free communion with heaven, causes the promises to send forth their sweet perfume, and death to appear only as a pleasant sleep. The shadows of coming evil fly away before the blessed light that streams down upon the soul from that world, where the aged pilgrim shall soon find his glorious rest.

And these consolations, which the gospel imparts to all believers, may in some respects be peculiarly precious to aged saints. The new-born soul rejoices in the glow of his first love; the saint of larger experience discovers yet new beauty and blessedness in Christ; but for the aged pilgrim in whom grace has assiduously wrought, and patience had her perfect work, are reserved richer clusters from the living Vine, riper and of sweeter flavor. To him belongs that peace which flows like a river with its calm and even tide—a peace which is the result of a long experience of the faithfulness of God. He has learned, as the younger Christian has not, to go at once to his Redeemer when sorrows rise or temptations assail—to live by faith on the Son of God. The loss of earthly friends, the withering of earthly hopes, the prospect of a speedy breaking up of all earthly connexions, even a deeper insight into the corruption of his nature, have all caused him to cling to Christ with increasing love.

A quiet home, kind friends, and a pecuniary competence may help to smooth the declining pathway, but amid all these, and incomparably beyond them, and even wholly apart from them, amid sickness, poverty, dependence, and neglect, Jesus, dwelling in the aged heart, is its richest source of peace.   He diffuses around the infirm and afflicted saint the atmosphere of heaven He commands, and the soul is still.   He is its sanctuary, into which it can run and hide from the griefs and cares of earth.   Upon his bosom, the bosom of infinite love, the weary head can be softly pillowed.   The legitimate influence of faith in Jesus Christ is a heavenly tranquillity of mind.   Aged disciple! Is this peace in its fulness not yet yours to enjoy?   We would direct you to Jesus   Beneath the Cross, as under the cool shadow of a great rock in a weary land, may the pilgrim repose after the burden and heat of life's earlier days, and calmly await his summons to the " better land."

PROVIDENCE hath a thousand keys to open a thousand doors for the deliverance of his own.— *Rutherford.*

DUTIES AND EVENTS.

DUTIES are ours, events are the Lord's ; when our faith goeth to meddle with events, and to hold a court (if I may so speak) upon God's providence, and beginneth to say, " How wilt thou do this and that ?" we lose ground ; we have nothing to do there, it is our part to let the Almighty exercise his own office, and steer his own helm ; there is nothing left us but to see how we may be approved of him, and how we may roll the weight of our weak souls in well doing upon him who is God omnipotent ; and when what we thus essay miscarrieth, it shall neither be our sin nor error.—*Rutherford.*

THESE are the days of the years of Abraham's life which he lived, a hundred threescore and fifteen years. Then Abraham gave up the ghost, and died in a good old age, an old man, and full of years ; and was gathered to his fathers.— *Genesis* xxv. 7, 8.

THE LOVE OF CHRIST.

WE want nothing but faith in stronger exercise to make us cheerful and comfortable under all the actual and possible changes of this poor life. Have we not a Saviour, a shepherd full of compassion and tenderness ? If we wish for love in a friend, he has shown love unspeakable ; he left his glory, assumed our nature, and submitted to shame, poverty, and death, even the death of the cross, that he might save us from sin and misery, and open the kingdom of heaven to us who were once his enemies. For he saw and pitied us when we knew not how to pity ourselves. If we need a powerful friend, Jesus is almighty; our help is in him who made heaven and earth, who raises the dead, and hushes the tempest's raging waves into a calm with a word. If we need a present friend, a help at hand in the hour of trouble, Jesus is always near, about our path by day, and our bed by night; nearer than the light by which we see, or the air we breathe; nearer than we are to ourselves; so that not a thought, a sigh, or a tear, escapes his notice. Since then his love and wisdom are infinite, and he has already done so much for us, shall we not trust him to the end? His mercies are countless as the sands, and hereafter we shall see cause to count our trials among our chief mercies. He sees there is a need-be for them, or we should not have them, and he has promised to make all things work together for our final good.—*John Newton, (when seventy-six years old.)*

GOD'S FAITHFULNESS

THERE are many Christians like young sailors, who think the shore and the whole land do move, when the ship and they themselves are moved; just so, not a few imagine that God moveth, and faileth, and changeth places, because their godly souls are subject to alteration; but the foundation of the Lord abideth sure.—*Rutherford.*

I HAVE been young, and now am old; yet have I not seen the righteous forsaken, nor his seed begging bread.—*Psalm* xxxvii. 25.

THOU art my hope, O Lord God: thou art my trust from my youth.—*Psalm* lxxi. 5.

THE dread and dislike of death by no means prove that a person is not a child of God. Even a strong believer may be afraid to die. We are not fond of handling a serpent, even though its sting is drawn.—*Martin.*

IMPORTANCE OF EXERCISE.

OLD age is called the winter of life, and with it are associated pain, infirmity, and sorrow.

The aged have lost the elasticity and freshness of earlier days. They are gradually sinking beneath the inevitable law that dooms man to the dust. Their sun is setting; the night draweth on.

Under these circumstances, they are sometimes disposed to withdraw entirely from active pursuits, and give themselves up to an indolent repose. They feel the need of rest and quiet in the evening of life; and surely they, if any, should enjoy this blessing. But they should never forget that the due exercise of mind and body is indispensable to happiness. Age brings no necessary exemption from this benevolent law. Said John Newton, in his seventieth year, "We must *work* while it is day, for the night cometh." And he was himself an example of the happy influence upon the health and happiness, of his own precept.

We would not here recommend severe and protracted toil, but only regular and moderate exercise, in connexion with some pleasing and useful employment. This accords with the laws of our being, whether in youth or age. It affords a healthful invigoration and refreshment. It tends most happily to draw the mind away from that melancholy brooding over real or fancied ills, which dries up the fountain of life and joy within the soul, and in which the unemployed, especially in advanced years, are prone to indulge.

It is common to hear men talk of retiring from business, to enjoy at their leisure the fruits of previous toil. But such an expectation generally ends in disappointment. The pleasure so fondly anticipated in a freedom from toil and care, comes not at the bidding. A feeling of uncomfortable lassitude and impatience ensues. The elegant home, with its pleasant arrangements, its shady walks, its cool retreats, whatever taste and wealth can furnish for embellishment and comfort, is irksome to its possessor, and he almost sighs for the bustle and bondage he has left. And there is nothing strange in this. It is the natural result of a violent transition, and of the transgression of that law which makes us happy only as our powers are duly exercised.

It would be better far that, instead of a sudden withdrawal, as age approaches, from the accustomed routine of labor, whether on the farm, in

the shop, the family, the pulpit, or whatever calling, there should be still such a continuance of
effort as is proportioned to the gradually declining strength.   And we may remark, by the way,
that such a course would not only greatly con-
duce to happiness, but to Christian usefulness.
It is by no means true that a moderate attention
even to worldly business, of necessity interferes
with spiritual enjoyment and devotedness.   We
may be diligent in business, and yet fervent in
spirit, serving the Lord.   And activity tends to
avert that lassitude and dulness, that spiritual
depression and decay of mind and body, which
are such powerful hindrances to usefulness.

If advanced years bring increased leisure, how
well for the aged, as well honoring to God,
that it be employed in his direct service.   What
a delightful field of activity is here opened before
the Christian in the evening of life !   How pleasing to see him, as he gradually retires from
worldly pursuits, turning with increased affection
to the church, which has had his earlier love-!
Here his mind may be exercised according to
the measure of its ability, and in the way most
favorable to that calm and holy repose so desir-

able for the aged. In the exercises of devotion, in spiritual conversation, in ministering the sweet charities of the gospel to the poor, and sick, and needy of the flock, and in other ways seeking the interests of the church and the religious welfare of the community, as he has opportunity or ability, the aged saint would renew his strength ; though old he would still be young. Many such we can recall to mind, whose labors of love have made them the glory of our churches. They bear fruit in old age. They are fair and flourishing. Their hoary head, found thus in the ways of righteousness, is a crown of glory. And while they honor God, he honors and blesses them. From not a few of the evils incident to age are they, in a measure or wholly, preserved.

Even when the saint, through extreme infirmity, is a "prisoner of the Lord" at home, he may exercise his mind, and brighten his declining days, by nurturing the "hidden life" of piety, by continual prayers for the church, and by devout conversation. Such an earnest devotion to God, so long as the ability is granted, will prove a refreshing cordial to the soul. And that cheerfulness which is connected with the spirit of benevolence, is one of the sources of a vigorous old age.

Familiar converse with the writings of the good and gifted will afford a pleasing exercise to the mind amid growing infirmities. Here, while the strength fails, the mind may be renewed day by day. Beside the fountains of holy thought and feeling, which God has opened in the works of those whom he has endowed to become teachers and comforters to their race, may the aged pilgrim sit and be refreshed. Here, by his fireside, what a noble company he may gather round him! with what glorious thoughts hold communion!

I have now in mind an aged saint, bent beneath the burden of more than fourscore years, a plain uneducated woman, moving in a humble sphere, but favored with an excellent understanding, to whom a book, and especially the " book of books," was an unfailing companion. By this habitual communion with the pure and great, her mind, through the blessing of God, retained to the last almost the sprightliness of youth, even when the frail body was bowed and ready to fail. Well do I remember how her eye would kindle when she was presented with a new religious book; and the sublime views she would express of the majesty of God, the preciousness of the Saviour, and the glory of heaven, were a pleasing proof of the happy influence of the practice we recommend;—for who can doubt that a premature decay of mental vigor would have resulted from the opposite course? Exercise, with the divine blessing, enabled her to maintain a vigorous life even to the borders of eternity.

When the sight at last grows dim, then highly favored is the aged Christian, to whom some loving voice conveys those thoughts which his eyes can no longer trace upon the printed page. And the aged should, if possible, enjoy this daily privilege. Without it, we have known them to spend their last days in sadness, and suffer a premature decay.

If at length the mind of the aged saint becomes too weak to follow even the reading of a book, let him fix his thoughts on Jesus. The contemplation of his love will warm the heart, and enkindle the mind, even when enfrosted by extreme old age.

7*

But heart and flesh at last must fail, the earth-ly tabernacle be dissolved. Then will the saint leave behind for ever the weakness of earth, and in a glorious and perpetual youth serve the "Lord who bought him." In that blessed world above, there is continual service. The lofty powers of saints and angels are ever exercised in loving, praising, and doing the will of, their Creator.

EXPERIENCE OF AN AGED BELIEVER.

THOUGH I am at present in good health, the question of Pharaoh to Jacob ought to be much in my thoughts, "How old art thou?" Indeed, I am old enough to be wiser and better than I am. Now I am turned of threescore, I have no right to expect that my abilities either for preach-ing or writing will continue very long. The shadows of evening cannot be very distant from me. It is therefore probable that the " Messiah " will be my last book from the press, and if so, I take leave of the public with a noble subject. Surely I am bound to wish that while my lips or my fingers can move, His name and His grace should employ my thoughts, my words, and my pen; and especially my last words, whether in the pulpit, in the parlor, or in my bed, and so from the press. What do I live for, but to bear a frequent public testimony to Him, and to commend him to my fellow-creatures?

I long to attain a habit of living with the Lord by the day; to depend no more upon to-morrow than yesterday; to hold myself in constant readiness; to be willing to go at a minute's warning, and leave all behind me in His hands, or (if such were his appointment) to be willing to stay and see those whom I love go before me. To be thus united to His will, and to rejoice in Him under any possible change, would be an attainment indeed! Perhaps none of us can fully reach it till we arrive at the threshold of glory. However, we may approach nearer and nearer to such a frame of mind, and every step towards it is preferable to thousands of gold and silver.—*John Newton. (Aged Pilgrim's Triumph.)*

JOHN NEWTON IN HIS OLD AGE.

It was with a mixture of delight and surprise that the friends and hearers of this eminent servant of God beheld him bringing forth such a measure of fruit in extreme old age. Though then almost eighty years old, his sight nearly gone, and incapable, through deafness, of joining in conversation; yet his public ministry was regularly continued, and maintained with a considerable degree of his former animation. His memory indeed was observed to fail, but his judgment in divine things still remained · and though some depression of spirits was observed, which he used to account for from his advanced age, yet his perception, taste, and zeal for the truth which he had long received and taught, were evident. Like Simeon, having seen the salvation of the Lord, he now only waited and prayed to depart in peace.

After Mr. Newton was turned of eighty, some of his friends feared he might continue his public ministrations too long. They marked not only his infirmities in the pulpit, but felt much on account of the decrease of his strength, and of his occasional depressions. Conversing with him in January, 1806, on the latter, he observed that he had experienced nothing which in the least affected the principles he had felt and taught; that his depressions were the natural result of *fourscore years*, and that, at any age, we can only enjoy that comfort from our principles which God is pleased to send. " But," replied I, " in the article of public preaching, might it not be best to consider your work as done, and stop before you evidently discover you can speak no longer ?" " I cannot stop," said he, raising his voice,—" *What! shall the old African blasphemer stop while he can speak ?*"

In every future visit, I perceived old age making rapid strides. At length his friends found some difficulty in making themselves known to him; his sight, his hearing, and his recollection exceedingly failed; but being mercifully kept from pain, he generally appeared easy and cheerful. Whatever he uttered was perfectly consistent with the principles which he had so long and so honorably maintained. Calling to see him a few days before he died, with one of his most intimate friends, we could not make him recollect either of us; but seeing him afterwards when sitting up in his chair, I found so much intellect remaining, as produced a short and affectionate reply, though he was utterly incapable of conversation.

Mr. Newton declined in this very gradual way,

till at length it was painful to ask him a question, or to attempt to rouse faculties almost gone; still his friends were anxious to get a word from him to learn the state of his mind in his latest hours.

About a month before his death, Mr. Smith's niece was sitting by him, to whom he said, "It is a great thing to die; and when heart and flesh fail, to have God for the strength of our heart, and our portion for ever. I know whom I have believed, and he is able to keep that which I have committed unto him against that great day. Henceforth there is laid up for me a crown of righteousness, which the Lord, the righteous Judge, shall give me at that day."

When Mrs. Smith came into the room, he said, "I have been meditating on a subject: 'Come and hear, all ye that fear God, and I will declare what he hath done for my soul.'"

At another time he said, "More light, more love, more liberty. Hereafter I hope, when I shut my eyes on the things of time, I shall open them in a better world. What a thing it is to live under the shadow of the wings of the Almighty! I am going the way of all flesh."

And when one replied, " The Lord is gracious," he answered, "If it were not so, how could I dare to stand before him ?"

The Wednesday before he died, when asked if his mind was comfortable, he replied, 'I am satisfied with the Lord's will." He seemed sensible to his last hour, but expressed nothing remarkable after these words. He departed December 31st, 1807, in the 83d year of his age. —*Memoir of Rev. John Newton, by Rev. Richard Cecil.*

THE AGED SERVING GOD.

MAY the old servants of God be dismissed from waiting on him ? No; their attendance is still required, and shall be still accepted; they shall not be cast off by their master in time of old age. Therefore, let not them desert his service. When, through the infirmities of age, they can no longer be working servants in God's family, yet they may be waiting servants. Those that, like Barzillai, are unfit for the entertainments of the courts of earthly princes, may yet relish the pleasures of God's courts as much as ever.

The Levites, when they were past the age of

fifty, and were discharged from the toilsome part of their ministrations, yet still must wait on God, must be quietly waiting to give honor to him, and to receive comfort from him. Those that have done the will of God, and their well-doing is at an end, have need of patience to enable them to wait till they inherit the promise; and the nearer the happiness is which they are waiting for, the dearer should the God be they are waiting on, and hope shortly to be with eternally.—*Matthew Henry.*

DO SOMETHING.

There is nothing more troublesome to a good mind than to do nothing. For besides the furtherance of our estate, the mind doth both delight and better itself with exercise. There is but this difference then betwixt labor and idleness, that labor is a profitable and pleasant trouble; idleness, a trouble both unprofitable and comfortless. I will be ever doing something; that either God when he cometh or Satan when he tempteth, may find me busied. And yet, since—as the old proverb is—better it is to be idle than effect nothing, I will not more hate doing nothing, than doing something to no purpose. I shall do good but a while; let me strive to do it while I may. —*Bishop Hall.*

RIGHT USE OF WEALTH.—The world teacheth me that it is madness to leave behind me those goods that I may carry with me; Christianity teacheth me that what I charitably give alive I carry with me dead: and experience teacheth me that what I leave behind I lose. I will carry that treasure with me, by giving it, which the worldling loseth, by keeping it: so, while his corpse shall carry nothing but a winding-sheet to his grave, I shall be richer under the earth than I was above it.—*Bishop Hall.*

BENEFIT OF AFFLICTION.

AM I afflicted? It is a Father's correcting hand. Am I in want? He knoweth it, and says, "The world is mine and the fulness thereof." Am I in the valley of humiliation? There grows the lily of the valley; and there, blessed be the God of all grace, have I found that lily, and derive thence such invigorating sweetness as none but myself can know. Would I exchange my pain, my restless nights, nay, even, sometimes, heart-sinkings, with the alternative of losing these heavenly bestowments? No! not to be made empress of the world. These are but means of pulling down the walls of the prison house, from whence the captive spirit shall soon wing its way to those realms of bliss, which it is now exploring with feeble faith and strong desire.—*Mrs. Hawkes.*

If I cannot *take pleasure in infirmities,* I can sometimes feel the profit of them. I can conceive a king to pardon a rebel, and take him into his family, and then say, " I appoint you, for a season, to wear a fetter. At a certain season, I will send a messenger to knock it off. In the meantime, this fetter will serve to remind you of your state : it may humble you, and restrain you from rambling."—*Newton.*

Cast me not off in the time of old age; forsake me not when my strength faileth.—*Psalm* lxxi. 9.

O God, thou hast taught me from my youth:

and hitherto have I declared thy wondrous
works.   Now also when I am old and grey-
headed, O God, forsake me not; until I have
showed thy strength unto this generation, and
thy power to every one that is to come.——
Psalm lxxi. 17, 18.

THE DEVOUT MAN.

A DEVOUT man is he that ever sees the Invisible, and ever trembleth before that God he sees ;
that walks even here on earth with the God of
heaven, and still adores that majesty with whom
he converses ; that confers hourly with the God
of spirits in his own language, yet so as no
familiarity can abate of his awe, nor fear abate
aught of his love : to whom the gates of heaven
are ever open, that he may go in at pleasure to
the throne of grace, and none of the angelical
spirits can offer to challenge him of too much
boldness ; whose eyes are well acquainted with
those heavenly guardians, the presence of whom
he doth as truly acknowledge as if they were his
sensible companions.   He is well known of the
King of Glory for a daily suitor in the court of

heaven; and none so welcome there as he—
Bishop Hall.

HUMAN FRAILTY.—Our frail bodies are tottering habitations; every beat of the heart is a rap
at the door, to tell us of our danger.—*Old Hum-
phrey.*

GLORY OF HEAVEN.

THE glory of the heaven which the gospel
prepares us for, which faith leads us to, which
the souls of believers long after, as that which
shall give us full rest, satisfaction, and complacency, is the full, open, perfect manifestation of
the glory, of the wisdom, goodness, and love of
God in Christ, in his person and mediation, with
the revelation of all his counsels concerning
them, and the communication of their effects to
us.

To have the eternal glory of God in Christ,
with all the fruits of his wisdom and love, whilst
we are ourselves under the full participation of
the effects of them, immediately, directly revealed
to us in a divine and glorious light, our souls
being furnished with a capacity to behold and

perfectly comprehend them ; this is the heaven which, according to God's promise, we look for. It is true, that there are sundry other things in particular that belong to this state of glory ; but what we have mentioned is the fountain of them all.

The whole of the glory of the state above is expressed by being ever with the Lord ; where he is, to behold his glory.   For in and through him is the beautiful manifestation of God and his glory made for evermore : and through him are all inward communications of glory to us.   Therefore, if we are spiritually minded, we should fix our thoughts on Christ above, as the centre of all heavenly glory.—*Owen on Spiritual-Mindedness.*

RELIEF FOR WANDERING THOUGHTS.

Some will say that there is not anything in all their duty towards God, wherein they are more at a loss than they are in this one, of fixing or exercising their thoughts on things heavenly or spiritual.   They acknowledge it a duty : they see an excellency in it with inexpressible usefulness But though they often attempt it, they cannot attain to anything but what makes them ashamed both of it and themselves. Their minds, they find, are unsteady, apt to rove and wander, or give entertainment to other things, and not to abide on the object which they design their meditation towards. On these considerations, ofttimes they are discouraged to enter on the duty, ofttimes give it over so soon as it is begun, and are glad if they come off without being losers by their endeavors, which often befalls them.

When you find yourselves perplexed and entangled, not able comfortably to persist in spiritual thoughts to your refreshment, take these two directions for your relief.

1. Cry and sigh to God for help and relief. Bewail the darkness, weakness, and instability of your minds, so as to groan within yourselves for deliverance. And if your designed meditations do issue only in a renewed gracious sense of your own weakness and insufficiency, with application to God for supplies of strength, they are by no means lost as unto a spiritual account. The thoughts of Hezekiah, in his meditations. did not seem to have any great order or consis-

tency, when he so expressed them; "Like a crane or a swallow, so did I chatter : I did mourn as a dove: mine eyes failed with looking upwards; O Lord, I am oppressed, undertake for me." When the soul labors sincerely for communion with God, but sinks into broken and confused thoughts under the weight of its own weakness, yet if he looks to God for relief, his chattering and mourning will be accepted with God, and profitable to himself.

2. Supply the brokenness of your thoughts with ejaculatory prayers. So was it with Hezekiah; when his meditations were weak and broken, he cried out in the midst of them, " O Lord, I am oppressed, undertake for me."

Lastly, Be not discouraged with an apprehension that all you can attain to in the discharge of this duty, is so little, so contemptible, as that it is to no purpose to persist in it. Nor be wearied with the difficulties you meet with in its performance. You have to do with him only in this matter, who will not break the bruised reed, nor quench the smoking flax; whose will is that none should despise the day of small things. And if there be in this duty a ready mind, it is accepted, according to what a man hath, and not according to what he hath not. He that can bring into this treasury only the mites of broken desires and ejaculatory prayers, so they be his best, shall not come behind them who cast into it out of their great abundance of ability and skill. —*Owen on Spiritual-Mindedness.*

LOVE.

*   *   *   *   *

The autumn of love
   Is the season of cheer—
Life's mild Indian summer,
   The smile of the year ;
Which comes when the golden,
   Ripe harvest is stored ;
And yields its own blessings—
   Repose and reward.

The winter of love
   Is the beam that we win,
While the storm scowls without,
   From the sunshine within.
Love's reign is eternal,
   The heart is his throne,
And he has all seasons
   Of life for his own.—*Morris.*

WHICH IS THE HAPPIEST SEASON?

At a festal party of old and young, the question was asked, which season of life was the most happy? After being freely discussed by the guests, it was referred for answer to the host, upon whom was the burden of fourscore years. He asked if they had noticed a grove of trees before the dwelling, and said, " When the spring comes, and in the soft air the buds are breaking on the trees, and they are covered with blossoms, I think, *How beautiful is Spring!* And when the summer comes, and covers the trees with its heavy foliage, and singing birds are all among the branches, I think, *How beautiful is Summer!* When autumn loads them with golden fruit, and their leaves bear the gorgeous tint of frost, I think, *How beautiful is Autumn!*   And when it is *sere* winter, and there is neither foliage nor fruit, then I look up, and through the leafless branches, as I could never until now, I see the *stars* shine through."—*Dr. Adams.*

CHRIST THE MEDIATOR.

Live by faith in the Lord Jesus Christ. We cannot with any confidence wait upon God but in and through a Mediator, for it is by his Son that God speaks to us, and hears from us; all that passes between a just God and poor sinners must pass through the hands of that blessed "Daysman who has laid his hand upon them both;" every prayer passes from us to God, and every mercy from God to us, by that hand It is in the face of the anointed that God looks upon us; and in the face of Jesus Christ that we behold the glory and grace of God shining. It is by Christ that we have access to God, and success with him in prayer, and therefore must make mention of his righteousness, even of his only. And in that habitual attendance we must be all the day living upon God; we must have an habitual dependence on him, who always appears in the presence of God for us, always gives attendance to be ready to introduce us.—*M. Henry.*

THOUGHTS OF GOD

DEATH will bring us all to God, to be judged by him; it will bring all the saints to him, to the vision and fruition of him; and one we are hastening to, and hope to be for ever with we are concerned to wait upon, and to cultivate an acquaintance with. Did we think more of death we should converse more with God. Our dying daily is a good reason for our worshipping daily; and therefore, wherever we are, we are concerned to keep near to God, because we know not where death will meet us. If we continue waiting on God and all the day long, we shall grow more experienced and expert in the great mystery of communion with God; and thus our last days will become our best days, our last works our best works, and our last comforts our sweetest comforts.—*M. Henry.*

THE SONG OF SEVENTY.

I AM not old—I cannot be old,
   Though threescore years and ten
Have wasted away, like a tale that is told,
   The lives of other men.

I am not old; though friends and foes
   Alike have gone to their graves,
And left me alone to my joys or my woes,
   As a rock in the midst of the waves.

I am not old—I cannot be old,
   Though tottering, wrinkled, and grey;

Though my eyes are dim, and my marrow is cold,
  Call me not old to-day.

For early memories round me throng,
  · Old times, and manners, and men,
As I look behind on my journey so long
  Of threescore miles and ten.

I look behind, and am once more young,
  Buoyant, and brave, and bold,
And my heart can sing, as of yore it sung,
  Before they called me old.

I do not see her—the old wife there—
  Shrivelled, and haggard, and grey,
But I look on her blooming, and soft, and fair,
  As she was on her wedding-day.

I do not see you, daughters and sons,
  In the likeness of women and men,
But I kiss you now as I kissed you once,
  My fond little children then.

And, as my own grandson rides on my knee,
  Or plays with his hoop or kite,
I can well recollect I was merry as he—
  The bright-eyed little wight.

'Tis not long since, it cannot be long,
  My years so soon were spent,
Since I was a boy, both straight and strong,
  Yet now am I feeble and bent.

A dream, a dream,—it is all a dream,
  A strange, sad dream, good sooth ,
For old as I am, and old as I seem,
  My heart is full of youth.

Eye hath not seen, tongue hath not told,
  And ear hath not heard it sung,
How buoyant and bold, though it seems to grow old,
  Is the heart, for ever young ;—

For ever young,—though life's old age
  Hath every nerve unstrung:
The heart, the heart, is a heritage
  That keeps the old man young !—*Tupper.*

FATHER AND SON.—How pleasant it is for a father to sit at his child's board ! It is like the aged man reclining under the shadow of the oak which he has planted.—*Walter Scott.*

VALUE OF RELIGION.

I ENVY no quality of the mind or intellect in others,—not genius, power, wit, or fancy ; but if I could choose what would be most delightful, and I believe most useful to me, I should prefer a firm religious belief to every other blessing, for it makes life a discipline of goodness, creates new hopes when all earthly hopes vanish, and throws over the decay, the destruction of existence, the most gorgeous of all lights : awakens life even in death, and from corruption and decay calls up beauty and divinity; makes an instrument of torture and of shame the ladder of ascent to paradise; and far above all combinations of earthly hopes, calls up the most delightful visions of palms and amaranths, the gardens of the blessed, the security of everlasting joys, where the sensualist and the sceptic view only gloom, decay, and annihilation.—*H. Davy.*

CHRIST'S LOVE TO HIS PEOPLE.

OBSERVE, O my soul, though thy celestial Bridegroom finds not in thee any merit, worthiness, or beauty, he will wash thee himself with his blood; he will adorn thee, and make thee truly amiable to himself and to his Father.

O sweet and eternal truth ! " He has loved us, and washed us from our sins in his own blood." Being clothed with his righteousness, we have more than angelical beauty.   If we have received the spirit of adoption, let us cleave to Christ alone, love him above all things, and walk in his commandments.   This is not only our duty, but a needful evidence of our sonship —*Bogatzky*.

OLD AGE.

Why should old age escape unnoticed here,
That sacred era to reflection dear?
That peaceful shore where passion dies away,
Like the last wave that ripples o'er the bay?
Oh! if old age were cancelled from our lot,
Full soon would man deplore the unhallowed blot?
Life's busy day would want its tranquil even,
And earth would lose its stepping-stone to heaven.

Caroline Gilman.

DISSUASIVES AGAINST A MURMURING SPIRIT.

Complainest thou, my soul, of thy long imprisonment, of thy long continued disappointment of escape from thy narrow, irksome cage? Faintest thou because thy labor is not over, nor the battle won? Rather humble thyself, and put thy mouth in the dust, that with all that has been done for thee, thou hast done so little thyself towards obtaining a meetness for thy heavenly inheritance. Were the corn fully ripe, it would be gathered into the garner. Thou art not ripened yet. Besides, were there no other reasons why thou shouldst wait patiently, it is enough that it is the will and good pleasure of thy Heavenly Father. Hast thou no obligations to him (whose thou art by creation, redemption, adoption, preservation), for mercies temporal and spiritual, through a whole life? Gird up the loins of thy mind, and say, " What shall I render unto the Lord for all his benefits?" Nothing canst thou render in a way of *merit;* but *every-thing* in doing and suffering according to his will. —*Mrs. Hawkes.*

THE DISCONSOLATE SAINT ENCOURAGED.

" WHY art thou cast down, O my soul?" when the speedy return of every birth-day should make thee glad that thou art one year nearer to the haven of rest, where thou hast so long desired to be. Has any new thing happened unto thee! anything that is not common to old age—common for an afflicted pilgrim, with a vile body of sin and death, to encounter and endure? Art thou not content to bear the breakings up of nature, with the drying up of its springs; and to walk through the valley of the shadow of death as those with whom, in former times, thou hast had sweet society, even when health and vigor were decayed, and when, with tottering steps and many a groan, they waited for that deliverance which they have now obtained? Dost thou expect that a new way is to be made for thee, instead of the royal way ordained for all pilgrims to the holy city? Look at thy dear relatives,—mother, brother, sisters, and others,—and again say, "Why art thou cast down, O my soul, and why art thou disquieted within me? Hope thou in God, for I shall yet praise him, who is the health of my countenance and my God."—*Mrs. Hawkes.*

THE PEASANT ON THE WELSH MOUNTAINS.

IT is told of a poor peasant on the Welsh mountains, that month after month, year after year, through a long period of declining life, he was used every morning, as soon as he awoke, to open his casement window towards the east, and look out to see if Jesus Christ was coming. He was no calculator, or he need not have looked so long; he was a student of prophecy, or he would not have looked at all; he was ready, or he would not have been in so much haste; he was willing, or he would rather have looked another way; he loved, or it would not have been the first thought of the morning. His master did not come, but a messenger did, to fetch the ready one home; the same preparation sufficed for both, the longing soul was satisfied with either.

Often, when in the morning the child of God awakes, wearily, and encumbered with the flesh; perhaps from troubled dreams; perhaps with troubled thoughts, his Father's secret comes presently across him; he looks up, if not out, to feel if not to see the glories of that last morning when the trumpet shall sound, and the dead shall arise indestructible: no weary limbs to bear the spirit down; no feverish dreams to haunt the visions; no dark forecasting of the day's events, or returning memory of the griefs of yesterday.—*Fry.*

PASSING UNDER THE ROD.

I saw when a father and mother had leaned
  On the arms of a dear cherished son,
And the star in the future grew bright in their gaze,
  As they saw the proud place he had won;
And the fast coming evening of life promised fair
  And its pathway grew smooth to their feet,

And the star-light of Love glimmered bright at the end,
  And the whispers of Fancy were sweet;—
But I saw when they stood bending low o'er the grave
  Where their hearts' dearest hope had been laid,
And the-star had gone down in the darkness of night,
  And joy from their bosoms had fled.
But the Healer was there, and his arms were around,
  And he led them with tenderest care,
And he showed them a star in the bright upper world—
  'Twas *their star* shining brilliantly there!
They had each heard a voice—'twas the voice of their God,
  "I love thee, I love thee—pass under the rod!"

M. S. B. Dana.

THE BIBLE.

O THOU Bible! holy book of wonders! what more can we need, when He who bears "the key of David" opens to us thy treasures? Where is the darkness which thy light will not dispel? where the emptiness which thy tree of life will not satisfy? where the thirst which thy living streams will not quench? where the mountains which cannot be ascended, when we have with us thy rod and staff? O Word of God! sent from heaven, who can estimate the fulness of that service of love which thou hast wrought for us? We seek after God—thou unveilest to us his face

We desire to know his will—thou discoverest to us his law, with its thunders and lightnings. Terrified by the voice from Sinai, we inquire into the state of our hearts—thou disclosest to us their most secret depths. We sink under the heavy load of our sins—thou showest to us the sentence of condemnation torn asunder, and nailed to the Saviour's cross. We tremble to find that we are naked in the presence of a holy God—thou tellest us of the spotless righteousness of Immanuel, and sayest gently, "Go in peace." We fear lest we should not walk worthy of our calling—thou sayest to us, "Take courage; for Christ is made of God unto you wisdom, and righteousness, and sanctification, and redemption." We tremble before the enemy who would fain swallow us up—again thou raisest our heads: "The Lion of the tribe of Judah hath conquered; take courage, take courage." Trouble surrounds us—thou liftest us out of the abyss: see, it was the chastisement of love. We are left alone—thou directest us to a friendly bosom, where all tears are wiped away. The path of our pilgrimage is dark and gloomy—thou givest us the wings of hope, so that we fly away over this world's mountains. The day of our life is coming to a close, the evening is drawing nigh—thou openest to us a window that looketh to the east, and behold, we see in the distance the glorious lights of our own eternal, and oh, what a house! O Word of Life! treasure of salvation! without equal; which makes our poverty rich, our weakness strong, gilding with heavenly light the shades of our earthly pilgrimage! let us kiss thee with kisses of love—let us cover thee with tears of joy. —*F. W. Krummacher.*

> "E'en down to old age all my people shall prove
> My sovereign, eternal, unchangeable love;
> And when hoary hairs shall their temples adorn,
> Like lambs in my bosom they still shall be borne."

A Lesson of Faith.—Wouldst thou know, O parent, what is that faith which unlocks heaven! Go not to wrangling polemics, but draw to thy bosom thy little one, and read in that clear, trusting eye the lessons of eternal life. Be only to thy God as thy child is to thee, and all is done! Blessed shalt thou be, indeed—" a little child shall lead thee!"

Baynham, the blessed martyr, when at the stake, said, " O ye Papists, you talk of miracles; behold here a true one: these flames are to me *a bed of roses.*"—*Lye.*

An aged man's voice has its beauties, though it is weak and low.—*Cicero.*

MY FATHER'S GRAVE.

It is well for the Christian that the arrangement of his lot is in better hands than his own. All that relates to life or death he may gratefully leave to him who holds the keys of both. But, were it lawful to express a choice, the position of the veteran, who, having fought the good fight, finishes his course in the possession of his faculties, and in the enjoyment of a hope full of immortality, would seem the happier portion. To have lived to some valuable purpose, and to have served their generation according to the will of God, may prove a source of holy satisfaction and delight to the servants of Christ, even when they rest from their labors and their works follow them.

" Then your lease is out," said one, as a venerable minister remarked that his days had exceeded threescore years and ten. "I never had a lease," that minister replied; "I was always a tenant at will, and I have often had warning to quit."

The final notice to that effect was delivered about two years afterwards, when, one morning, indications not easily mistaken assured him that the time of his departure was at hand. Perfectly calm and collected, he sent his sexton round the village to invite his little flock to come and see their pastor die. The last four hours of his life he spent in separately commending them "to God, and to the word of his grace;" and then, in the act of turning to find an easier posture, he fell asleep in Jesus.

Among some papers, the seal of which was not to be broken till his decease, was found a letter to his children, which, after alluding to some matters in relation to his will, closed with these words: "Press on: follow me to glory. YOUR FATHER BIDS YOU FAREWELL."

In the sanctuary where for two and forty years he labored for the glory of God and the salvation of men, his remains await the resurrection of the just.   And there has the writer, while weeping over the long flat stone which records his name, recalled the exclamation of Elisha: "My father! my father! the chariots of Israel, and the horsemen thereof!"—*D. E. Ford.*

BAXTER'S DYING WORDS.—The Rev. Richard Baxter, when near the close of his course, exclaimed, "I have pains—there is no arguing against sense; but I have peace, I *have* peace." "You are now drawing near your long desired home," said one. "I believe, I believe," was his reply. When asked, "How are you?" he promptly answered, "ALMOST WELL!"

THE OLD MAN'S FUNERAL.

I SAW an aged man upon his bier;
   His hair was thin and white, and on his brow
A record of the cares of many a year;—
   Cares that were ended and forgotten now.
And there was sadness round, and faces bowed,
And woman's tears fell fast, and children wailed aloud.

Then rose another hoary man, and said,
   In faltering accents, to that weeping train,

"Why mourn ye that our aged friend is dead ?
  Ye are not sad to see the gathered grain,
Nor when their mellow fruit the orchards cast,
Nor when the yellow woods shake down the ripened mast.

Ye sigh not when the sun, his course fulfilled,
  His glorious course, rejoicing earth and sky,
In the soft evening, when the winds are stilled,
  Sinks where his islands of refreshment lie,
And leaves the smile of his departure, spread
O'er the warm-colored heaven and ruddy mountain head.

Why weep ye, then, for him, who, having won
  The bound of man's appointed years, at last,
Life's blessings all enjoyed, life's labors done,
  Serenely to his final rest has passed :
While the soft memory of his virtues, yet
Lingers like twilight hues, when the bright sun is set ?"

Bryant.

BENEFITS OF AFFLICTION.

WHEN we pray for increase of faith and grace, and that we may have stronger proofs of our own sincerity, and of the Lord's faithfulness and care, we do but, in other words, pray for affliction. He is the best known and noticed in the time of trouble, as a present and all-sufficient help. How grand and magnificent is the arch over our heads in a starry night! But if it were always day, the stars could not be seen. The firmament of Scripture, if I may so speak, is spangled with exceeding great and precious promises, as the sky is with stars, but the value and beauty of many of them are only perceptible to us in the night of affliction.—*John Newton.*

THE HOSPITAL AND THE PALACE.

God's house is a hospital at one end, and a palace at the other. In the hospital end are Christ's members upon earth, conflicting with various diseases, and confined to a strict regimen of his appointing. What sort of a patient must he be, who would be sorry to be told that the hour is come for his dismission from the hospital, and to see the doors thrown wide open for his admission into the presence!—*Adam.*

NEARER HOME.

We are travelling in the coach of time; every day and hour brings us nearer home, and the coach-wheels whirl round apace when we are upon the road; we seldom think the carriage goes too fast; we are pleased to pass the mile-stones: I call new-year's day, or my birth-day, a mile-stone.

I have now almost reached my seventy-third yearly mile-stone; what dangers have I escaped or been brought through! If my heart would jump to be within three miles of you, why does it not jump from morning till night, to think that I am probably within three years of seeing the Lamb upon the throne, and joining in the praises of the blessed spirits of the redeemed, who behold him without a veil or a cloud, and are filled with his glory and love!—*John Newton.*

THE GOOD MAN'S CONSOLATION.

How numerous and how powerful are the consolations of a good man in the season of adversity! External reverses cannot rob him of that internal peace which he enjoys. From a state of opulence he may be reduced to a state of indigence, From a state of health he may be reduced to a state of bodily distress. His children may descend, one by one, before him into the tomb The friends of his bosom, with whom he had spent many a happy hour, may drop around him in the arms of death, like the withered leaves of a tree scattered on the ground by the autumnal blast. He himself may be doomed to drag out the scanty remains of a worn-out existence, bereft of comforts which he once enjoyed, and burdened with the infirmities of age. But has he no friend left to speak kindly to him? Has he none to soothe and to support him? Yes: he has One above, "that sticketh closer than a brother." He has a living Redeemer, and therefore does he sing in the season of adversity, "The Lord is my light and my salvation; whom shall I fear? The Lord is the strength of my life; of whom shall I be afraid? In the time of trouble he shall hide me in his pavilion; in the secret of his tabernacle shall he hide me: he shall set me upon a rock."—*M'Kerrow.*

CHRIST is a refiner's fire. We would like well enough to come and warm ourselves at this fire; but the business depends upon being thrown into it.—*Adam.*

AND when Abraham was ninety years old and nine, the Lord appeared to Abraham, and said unto him, I am the Almighty God: walk before me, and be thou perfect.—*Genesis* xvii. 1.

A THOUGHT OF THE PAST.

I woke from slumber at the dead of night,
   Stirred by a dream which was too sweet to last—
A dream of boyhood's season of delight;
   It flashed along the dim shapes of the past!
And, as I mused upon its strange appeal,
   Thrilling my heart with feelings undefined,
Old memories, bursting from Time's icy seal,
   Rushed, like sun-stricken fountains, on my mind
Scenes, among which was cast my early home,
   My favorite haunts, the shores, the ancient woods,
Where, with my schoolmates, I was wont to roam,
   Green, sloping lawns, majestic solitudes—
All rose to view, more lovely than of yore;
   They faded—and I wept—a child indeed once more!

Sargent.

SUBMISSION TO THE WILL OF GOD.

O what wisdom is it to believe and not to dispute; to submit our thoughts to God's court, and not to repine at any act of his justice! It is impossible to be submissive, if we stay our thoughts down among the confused rollings and wheels of second causes, as—" O the place! O the time! O if this had been, this had not followed! O the linking of this accident with this time and place!"—Look up to the master motion and the first wheel; see and read the decree of heaven and the Creator of men. "How unsearchable are his judgments, and his ways past finding out!"—*Rutherford.*

COMFORT IN AFFLICTION.

EVEN when a believer sees no light, he may feel some hope; when he cannot close with a promise, he may lay hold on an attribute, and say: Though both my flesh and my heart fail, yet divine faithfulness and divine compassion fail not. Though I can hardly discern at present either sun, moon, or stars, yet will I cast anchor in the dark, and ride it out, until the day break and the shadows flee away.—*Arrowsmith.*

BELIEVER, go on; your last step will be on the head of the old serpent; but crush it, and spring from it into glory.—*Mason.*

GOD hangs the greatest weights upon the smallest wires.—*Bacon.*

CALM, PEACE, AND LIGHT.

THERE is a Calm the poor in spirit know,
That softens sorrow and that sweetens woe ;
There is a Peace that dwells within the breast,
When all without is stormy and distressed ;
There is a Light that gilds the darkest hour,
When dangers thicken, and when tempests lower.
That Calm to faith, and love, and hope is given—
That Peace remains when all beside is riven—
That Light shines down to man direct from heaven !

FOOTSTEPS OF ANGELS.

WHEN the hours of day are numbered,
  And the voices of the night
Wake the better soul that slumbered,
  To a holy, calm delight :

Ere the evening lamps are lighted,
  And, like phantoms grim and tall,
Shadows from the fitful firelight
  Dance upon the parlor wall ;

Then the forms of the departed
  Enter at the open door,
The beloved ones, the true-hearted,
  Come to visit me once more ;

He, the young and strong, who cherished
  Noble longings for the strife,

By the road-side fell and perished,
  Weary with the march of life !

They, the holy ones and weakly,
  Who the cross of suffering bore,
Folded their pale hands so meekly,
  Spoke with us on earth no more .

And with them the being beauteous,
  Who unto my youth was given,
More than all things else to love me,
  And is now a saint in heaven.

With a slow and noiseless footstep
  Comes that messenger divine,
Takes the vacant chair beside me,
  Lays her gentle hand in mine.

And she sits and gazes at me
  With those deep and tender eyes,
Like the stars, so still and saintlike,
  Looking downward from the skies

Uttered not, yet comprehended,
  Is the spirit's voiceless prayer,
Soft rebukes in blessings ended,
  Breathing from her lips of air.

Oh ! though oft depressed and lonely,
  All my fears are laid aside,
If I but remember only
  Such as these have lived and died.—*Longfellow.*

IT is one of the melancholy pleasures of an old man to recollect the kindness of friends, whose kindness he shall experience no more.—*Dr. Johnson.*

THE HAPPY OLD MAN.

ONE stormy winter day, the Rev. Mr. Young, of Jedburgh, was visiting one of his people, an old man, who lived in great poverty in a lonely cottage. He found him sitting with the Bible open on his knees, but in outward circumstances of great discomfort—the snow drifting through the roof, and under the door, and scarce any fire on the hearth. "What are you about to-day, John?" was his question on entering. "Ah, sir," said the happy saint, "*I'm sitting under His shadow with great delight!*"—*Christian Treasury.*

THE CHRISTIAN'S GRAVE.

WHEN by a good man's grave I muse alone,
Methinks an angel sits upon the stone,
Like those of old, on that thrice hallowed night,
Who sate and watched in raiment heavenly bright;
And, with a voice inspiring joy, not fear,
Says, pointing upward, that he is not here,
That he is risen.—*Rogers.*

WE may sing even in our winter storm, in the expectation of a summer sun at the turn of the year.—*Rutherford.*

FRIENDS IN HEAVEN.

THE expectation of loving my friends in heaven, principally kindles my love to them on earth. If I thought I should never know them, and consequently never love them, after this life is ended, I should number them with temporal things, and only love them as such. But I now delightfully converse with my godly friends, in a firm persuasion that I shall converse with them for ever; and I take comfort in those that are dead or absent, as believing I shall shortly meet them in heaven; and I love them with an heavenly love, as the heirs of heaven, even with a love that shall there be perfected, and for ever exercised.—*Baxter.*

GOD hath many sharp-cutting instruments and rough files for the polishing of his jewels; and those he especially esteems, and means to make the most resplendent, he hath oftenest his tools upon.—*Leighton*

AFFLICTION SANCTIFIED.

METHINKS if ye would know
How visitations of calamity
Affect the pious soul, 'tis shown you here:
Look yonder at that cloud, which, through the sky
Sailing along, doth cross in her career
The rolling moon.   I watched it as it came,
And deemed the deep opaque would blot her beams;
But melting like a wreath of snow, it hangs
In folds of wavy silver round, and clothes
The orb with richer beauties than her own;
Then passing, leaves her in her light serene.—*Southey.*

THE journey through life is as Peter's walking on the water; and if Christ does not reach out his hand, we are every moment in danger of sinking.—*Adam.*

THE WORLDLING AND THE CHRISTIAN.

A GENTLEMAN once took a friend to the roof of his house, to show him the extent of his possessions.   Waving his hand about, " There," said he, " is my estate."   Pointing to a great distance on one side, " Do you see that farm? Well, that is mine."   Pointing again to the other side, " Do you see that house?   That also belongs to me." In turn, his friend asked, " Do you see that little village out yonder? Well, there lives a poor woman within that village who can say more than all this." " Ah ! what can she say ?" " Why, she can say, CHRIST IS MINE !" Indeed she was the richer of the two.

THE LAST DAYS OF DR. WATTS AND MR. HERVEY.

WHEN Dr. Watts was almost worn out and broken down by his infirmities, he observed, in conversation with a friend : " I remember an aged minister to say, that the most learned and knowing Christians, when they come to die, have only the same plain promises of the gospel for their support as the common and unlearned ; and so," said he, " I find it. It is the plain promises of the gospel that are my support ; and I bless God they are plain promises, that do not require much labor and pains to understand them ; for I can do nothing now but look into my Bible for some promise to support me ; I live upon that."

This was likewise the case with the pious and excellent Mr. Hervey. He writes, about two months before his death, " I now spend almost my whole time in reading and praying over the Bible." And again, to another friend, near the same time: "I am now reduced to a state of infant weakness, and given over by my physician. My grand consolation is to meditate on Christ; and I am hourly repeating those heart-reviving lines of Dr. Young :—

> This—only this—subdues the fear of death.
> And what is this? Survey the wondrous cure,
> And at each step let higher wonder rise!
> Pardon for infinite offence! And pardon
> Through means that speak its value infinite!
> A pardon bought with blood! With blood divine,
> With blood divine of Him I made my foe!
> Persisted to provoke! Though woo'd and awed,
> Bless'd and chastis'd, a flagrant rebel still!
> A rebel 'midst the thunders of his throne,
> Nor I alone! A rebel universe!
> My species up in arms! Not one exempt!
> Yet for the foulest of the foul He dies!
> Most joy'd for the redeem'd from deepest gulf!
> As if our race were held of highest rank,
> And Godhead dearer, as more kind to man.

I TRIED to make crooked things straight, till I have made these knuckles sore, and now I must leave it to the Lord.—*John Newton.*

THE CHRISTIAN'S PROSPECT.

As when the weary traveller gains
  The height of some o'erlooking hill,
His heart revives, if 'cross the plains
  He eyes his home, though distant still.

A traveller, after a long journey, when he is weary and faint, and sits down, if he see the town before him, it puts life into him, and he plucks up his feet, and resolves not to be weary till he be at his journey's end. O look at the crown and white robe set before you, and faint if you can ; get on the top of Mount Nebo—look on the land of promise—those good things set before you : taste the grapes of Canaan before you come to Canaan.—*Nalton.*

If an angel were sent to find the most perfect man, he would probably not find him composing a body of divinity, but perhaps a cripple in the poor-house, whom the parish wish dead, but humbled before God by far lower thoughts of himself than others think of him.—*John Newton.*

Live not upon the comforts of God, but upon the God of comforts.—*Mason.*

JESUS LIVES.

At death, earthly friendships are dissolved; with the friend our comforts die, and the satisfaction we enjoyed in their society leaves only a painful remembrance of the pleasures we have lost. But Jesus lives for ever! lives to make intercession for his friends above; to communicate constant supplies of grace to them below; to guide them through all the scenes of mortal life; to crown them with victory over the last enemy; and to bring them safe to his glorious presence to live with him for ever and ever! Happy, happy souls! who have an interest in this all-sufficient, this everlasting Friend! Blessed Jesus! teach me to know thee and to love thee more; let me hear the voice of thy sacred Spirit whispering to my heart that thou art mine; assure me of my interest in thy almighty, thy unchangeable love! then I shall be blest indeed. —*Mrs. Steele.*

AM I A CHRISTIAN?

"Examine yourselves whether ye be in the faith," says an inspired apostle. This duty, so important for all the professed disciples of Christ, is specially so for such of them as are advanced in years. A few more days, and the validity of their hopes for eternity must be tested in the immediate presence of the Searcher of hearts. Before him must they soon appear,—the Ancient of Days—whose " eyes are as a flame of fire," and whose decisions will be infallible and final.

These thoughts, says an aged professor, have often occupied my mind, while contemplating my swift approach to eternity, and again and again have I asked myself, Am I Christ's, or am I not ? Soon I must go hence,—am I prepared to depart in peace ?

With all affection, aged friend, we come to proffer our aid in this solemn examination. Let us confer together upon this all-important matter.

You have professed to be a child of God, and an heir of glory,—are you such, in truth ?

The Scriptures affirm, that except a man be born again, he cannot see the kingdom of God, and that he who believeth in Jesus shall be saved. If you, dear friend, have experienced that regeneration, and exercised that faith, they will have made that deep impression upon your heart, and character, and life, which will itself be a satisfactory witness. They are God's own work, and they bring with them their own testimony. The changes they effect are radical and permanent and holy. Permit us to inquire, then, Have you ever observed any essential change in your views and feelings upon the great themes of religion, or are they substantially the same that they ever were? Without asking you to refer to any particular day, or hour, or spot, we would ask, Were you ever disturbed by a sense of personal sinfulness and guilt, and of lying under the curse of God? Were you ever conscious of heartfelt sorrow, and of a feeling of deserved condemnation, for having sinned against a holy, good, and sovereign God? Did you ever commit your soul into the hands of Jesus, to be washed in his blood, and justified freely by his righteousness? Has a change been experienced so great, that you can say, Whereas I was blind, now I see—dead, but now I live? May it be compared to a new birth, a new creation in Christ? Can you ascribe it to a power no less than that of God?

And what have been its fruits? Have you

discovered in your heart a love to God and holiness, to which it was once a stranger?—a new love to the word of truth, to secret prayer, the communion of the saints, the worship of the sanctuary, and the precepts of Jesus Christ? Have the inward workings of sin occasioned deep contrition and self-loathing? and has likeness to Christ appeared in your eyes the most desirable of all things? Have you been accustomed to pray for the Holy Spirit to sanctify you wholly? Have you hungered and thirsted after righteousness? Have you mourned because your love to Christ and heavenly things was no more ardent? Have you felt a new love to all mankind, a spirit of forgiveness under injuries, and a peculiar affection for the disciples of Christ?

When tried, disappointed, bereaved, has your heart quietly submitted to the divine will, or if murmurs against providence then arose, have godly sorrow succeeded, and earnest prayer for a spirit of patient waiting upon God? Have you known the sweetness of resting upon the ! ord and trusting his promises? Have the thoughts of heaven cheered your pilgrimage? Has God at times appeared eminently glorious? the Saviour superlatively precious, and worthy of all acceptation? Has your whole experience led to a growing confidence in God's wisdom and love? Has it led to a deeper conviction of the exceeding sinfulness of your nature, of the deceitfulness of your heart, and of your constant dependence on the grace of God? Has it given double assurance to your belief in the alone possibility of salvation through the atoning sacrifice of the Son of God? And in contemplating your attainments in piety, do you say from the heart, By the grace of God I am what I am, and if I am ever saved, I shall be a sinner saved by grace.

If, aged friend, you can, with humble gratitude to God, give an affirmative answer to these inquiries, we encourage you to believe that you are a disciple of Christ, and that he will own you as such in the great day. Yes, he who has begun a good work in you, will carry it on until the day of Jesus Christ. He will not forsake your grey hairs. He will guide you by his counsel, and afterwards receive you to glory. With an aged saint now at rest, you may say, There is laid up for me a crown of righteousness, which the Lord, the righteous Judge, will give me. May the Lord grant you the full assurance of hope unto the end.

But here is another aged pilgrim who speaks a different language. His feelings are those of mingled confidence and distrust. He hopes and fears, rejoices and desponds by turns. He is so painfully conscious of sin and imperfection in all his feelings and services, that self-examination rather perplexes and discourages, than assures and comforts him. Oh, aged friend, thus writing bitter things against yourself, and almost ready to exclude yourself from any part in Christ's redeeming work, we would fain address to you a word of consolation. Be assured that there may be discerned in your exercises clear traces of the operation of divine grace. This tender conscience, this trembling solicitude, reveal, even amid the mists of unbelief, a heart that has mourned for sin, and that longs for freedom from its chains. The mere worldling is not conscious of such emotions. And yet you should deplore your deficiency of faith. Here probably lies the secret of your fears. You look too exclusively at your sinful heart, and forget the blessed, all-sufficient Saviour. It is from him that peace must come—from his wounds, his groans, his obedience, his death, his intercession. Behold him as having borne the burden of your guilt, and let your soul find rest. Consider that he, as your substitute and surety, has effected and guaranteed your salvation. To make the number and greatness of your sins a reason for despair, is to limit the infinite fulness of his merits. He can save unto the uttermost. By believing, you glorify the Son of God. He invites you. to believe. You are authorized, trembling one, on the word of God himself, to cast yourself as you are, immediately and wholly, upon the atonement of Christ, and to rejoice in hope of glory.

But oh, if these pages should meet the eye of one aged reader, to whom all that we have said is but a strange language, we would with all tenderness and plainness say to you, Dear friend, it is high time you had made your peace with God. Time presses on, death will soon be at the loor, your hoary head and trembling steps are warnings not to be mistaken that your account must soon be rendered. Are you prepared to meet God in judgment? Have you good reason to believe that your sins are forgiven through the merits of Christ, so that death would be gain? Alas, if you hope to enter heaven except through Him who is the "way," your hope' will fail. And if you are trusting in him without having mourned for sin, without having felt that you were lost unless he should pardon and accept you, your trust will prove delusive. It is the penitent, broken-hearted sinner, to whom Jesus says, Thy sins are forgiven thee. Such he invites to come to him, even at the eleventh hour. Such he will in no wise cast out. His merits are infinite. He can save unto the uttermost. His blood cleanseth from all sin. Oh, aged traveller, your sun soon will set. Shall it go down in gloom? Shall your feet stumble upon the dark mountains? Think of your long life, of its numberless mercies from helpless infancy to old age. These were all God's gifts. Have they been thankfully received? Have they led you to repentance? Sad account! A whole life of sin to answer for! God forgotten, the world loved, self regarded, Christ rejected! Aged sinner! your life may have been stained with no crime, but to forget God, to disobey God; this is

a criminal offence in the sight of heaven.
Quickly repent. To-day harden not your heart.
Now is the day of salvation. To-morrow may
be too late.

LETTER TO AN AGED PERSON.

MUCH honored sir :—Grace, mercy, and peace
be to you. I beseech you, sir, by the salvation
of your precious soul, and the mercies of God,
make good and sure work of your salvation, and
try upon what ground-stone you have builded.
Worthy and dear sir, if ye be upon sinking sand,
a storm of death and a blast will loose Christ and
you, and wash you off the rock! O for the
Lord's sake, look narrowly to the work. Read
over your life with the light of God's daylight
and sun. It is good to look to your compass,
and all you have need of, ere you take shipping ;
for no wind can blow you back again. Remember, when the race is ended, and the flag either
won or lost, and you are in the utmost circle and
border of time, and put your foot within the
march of eternity, all your good things of this

short night-dream shall seem to you like the
ashes of a blaze of thorns or straw, and your
poor soul shall be crying, Lodging, lodging, for
God's sake! Then shall your soul be more glad
at one of your Lord's lovely smiles, than if you
had the charters of three worlds for all eternity.
Let pleasures and gain, will and desires of this
world, be put over in God's hands, as arrested
goods, that you cannot claim. Now when you
are drinking the grounds of your cup, and are
upon the utmost ends of the last link of time,
and old age, like death's long shadow, is casting
a covering upon your days, it is no time to court
this vain life, and to set love and heart upon it:
it is near after supper; seek rest and ease for
your soul, in God through Christ. Come in,
come in to Christ, and see what you want, and
find it in him: he is the short cut, as we used to
say, and the nearest way to an out-gate of all
your burdens. I dare avouch, you shall be
dearly welcome to him. Angels' pens, angels'
tongues, nay, as many worlds of angels as there
are drops of water in all the seas and fountains
and rivers of the earth, cannot paint him out to
you. I think his sweetness, since I was a pri-

soner, has swelled upon me to the greatness of two heavens. O for a soul as wide as the utmost circle of the highest heaven that containeth all, to contain his love !—*Rutherford.*

THE EXPERIENCE OF JOHN NEWTON.

You kindly inquire after my health : myself and family are, through the divine favor, perfectly well; yet, healthy as I am, I labor under a growing disorder, for which there is no cure; I mean old age. I am not sorry it is a mortal disease, from which no one recovers : for who would live always in such a world as this, who has a Scriptural hope of an inheritance in the world of light? I am now in my seventy-second year, and seem to have lived long enough for myself. I have known something of the evil of life, and have had a large share of the good. I know what the world *can* do, and what it *cannot* do ; it can neither give nor take away that *peace of God which passeth all understanding ;* it cannot soothe a wounded conscience, nor enable us to meet death with comfort. . . . The Gospel is a catholicon adapted to all our wants and all our feelings, and a suitable help when every other fails.—*John Newton.*

HE who sends the storm steers the vessel.—*Adam.*

KNOW ye are as near heaven as ye are far from yourself, and far from the love of a bewitching world.—*Rutherford.*

FAITH is the better of the free air, and of the sharp winter storm in its face.—*Rutherford.*

THE TREMBLING CHRISTIAN.

IT is the duty of good people to labor after a holy security and serenity of mind, and to use the means appointed for the obtaining it. Give not way to the disquieting suggestions of Satan, and to those tormenting doubts and fears that arise in your own souls. Study to be quiet, chide yourself for your distrusts, charge yourselves to believe and to hope in God, that you may yet praise him. You are in the dark concerning yourselves; do as Paul's mariners did, cast anchor and wish for the day.

Poor, trembling Christian ! thou art tossed with tempests, and not comforted ; try to lay thee down in peace and sleep ; compose thyself into a sedate and even frame. In the name of Him whom winds and seas obey, command down thy tumultuous thoughts, and say, " Peace, be still." Lay that aching, trembling head of thine where the beloved disciple laid his, in the bosom of the Lord Jesus; or, if thou hast not yet attained such boldness of access to him, lay that aching, trembling head of thine at the feet of the Lord Jesus, by an entire submission to him, saying, " If I perish, I will perish here :" put it into his hand by an entire confidence in him ; submit it to his disposal, who knows how to speak to the heart. And if thou art not yet entered into this present rest that remaineth for the people of God, yet look upon it to be a land of promise, and, therefore, though it tarry, wait for it, for the vision is for an appointed time, and at the end it shall speak and shall not lie. " Light is sown for the righteous," and what is sown shall come up again at last in harvest of joy.—*M. Henry.*

THE AGED MINISTER.—" Well, father ———,' was once said to a servant of Christ when past fourscore years, " on the whole, do you think you shall go to heaven when you die ?"—His instant reply was, " Why, where else should I go ?" as if the question surprised him. So in harmony was his soul with God, and purity, and heaven, that he seemed instinctively to look upward for his eternal home.

THE AGED BELIEVER'S EXPERIENCE AND PROSPECTS.

[FROM A LETTER TO A FRIEND.]

LET it not be long before you inform me how you and all your family are. I hope the young ones grow and thrive like olive plants, and that the elder branches of the family are planted and planting in the Lord's vineyard, and promise to be trees of righteousness, and to bear fruit in their old age.

We are all much as we were, when we last saw you, only about a year and a month older: that is, so much the nearer to that gate which death will ere long open to introduce us to an eternal state. It is a solemn thought. How new and untried the passage! How inconceivable the prospect beyond it! Formerly I have supposed that if I lived beyond the age of sixty, the nearness and importance of that change which I might then reasonably expect could not be far off, would be continually upon my mind. But now that I am near sixty-three, I find myself little more affected by it than I was thirty years ago. I may now be sure, that if grace does not weaken my attachment to the things of time, an advance in years will not do it. I am an inconsistent creature, and should be condemned out of my own mouth by what I preach to others, if the Lord were strict to mark what is amiss. But I trust I am not under the law, but under grace. He knows my frame, that it is altogether shattered and defiled, and that I have no *plea* to offer in my own behalf; and therefore he has mercifully provided one for me, on which my soul desires wholly to rely. I have sinned, but Christ has died, has risen, and is exalted a Prince and a Saviour, and upon the warrant of his own word, I venture my all upon him. I could complain much of myself, but you cannot help me; therefore I forbear. I would rather invite you to join with me in praise. "Come, magnify the Lord with me, and let us exalt his holy name together." He found us when we sought him not; *then* we began to seek him, and *then* he was pleased to be found by us. He has guided us by his eye, guarded us by the way, restored us when wandering, revived us when fainting, healed us when wounded. He has known our souls in adversity, helped us in all our difficulties, comforted and supported us under all our sorrows. If we look around us, how are we distinguished by the mercies of his providence; our wants supplied, our wishes almost prevented, comforts and friends on every side, and the green pastures of his ordinances near and frequent, to the refreshment of our souls. If we look forward, what unspeakably greater blessings! We cannot conceive a thousandth part of what is signified by the white robes, the golden harp, the balm of life, the rivers of pleasure, which are prepared for the faithful followers of the Lamb! Can anything enhance the value of these blessings and these hopes, or heighten our obligations for them? Yes, the consideration of the way in which they become ours. The smallest and greatest of them are all the price of blood.—*John Newton.*

THE AGED AND THE YOUNG CHRISTIAN.

The old Christian, who has by grace reached a somewhat more elevated ground than one beginning the spiritual journey, should remember the toils, conflicts, weakness, darkness, temptations, and so forth, that made him groan and oftentimes ready to faint, in ascending to that point, that he may deal tenderly and gently with such as are yet laboring over the same ground. So desirous is the advanced Christian that others may have the same joy, that he is apt to forget there must first be the fight and the race. He calls on all to rejoice as he does; to be dead to the world as he is; to bathe in the sweet ocean of redeeming love, and to breathe freely in the pure element of holy communion. It is natural he should so speak; but this meat should be reserved for riper years; and the milk of younger experience should be given to babes. In this thing I have erred, and now would correct my mistake —*Mrs. Hawkes.*

THE DEATH OF A FRIEND.

O FRIEND, I stood beside thee at thy tomb,
Filled with a thousand bleeding memories;
Thine image rose upon my thoughts, and filled
My spirit with sad love. I thought, dear friend,
That in the strife of thy long suffering
I had not mourned enough for one so loved.
I then wept inly. But a thought returned,
As though an angel clothed in shining raiment
Stood by the opening tomb, and said, Weep not,
For *she* is not in dust, but far away,
Even with the deathless, where no pain can come—
Beyond the reach of sorrows. Then I looked
On those who stood with solemn aspect round,
And knew we were the dead in sin, not thou!
Thou art not of the dead : or if so named,
The tomb grows holy when we think of thee.
No more the cavern of decay from which
The bosom shrinks appalled—but holy—holy—
The sacred portal of the realm beyond
Where they who follow thee are found with God.

James Wills.

THE DEATH OF CHRIST.—Christ by his death slew for us our infernal foes; by it he abolished death; by death he destroyed him that had the power of death; by death he took away the sting of death; by death he made death a pleasant sleep to saints, and the grave for a while an easy house and home for the body.—*Bunyan.*

LET dissolution come when it will, it can do the. Christian no harm, for it will be but a passage out of a prison into a palace: out of a sea of troubles into a haven of rest; out of a crowd of enemies to an innumerable company of true, loving, and faithful friends; out of shame, reproach, and contempt, into exceeding great and eternal glory.—*Bunyan.*

HAPPINESS OF HEAVEN.

ONLY to be permitted to contemplate such a being as Jehovah, to see goodness, holiness, justice, mercy, long-suffering and sovereignty personified and condensed; to see them united with eternity, infinite power, unerring wisdom, omnipresence, and all-sufficiency; to see all these natural and moral perfections indissolubly united and blended in sweet harmony in a pure, spiritual being, and that being placed on the throne of the universe; I say, to see this, would be happiness enough to fill the mind of any creature in existence. But in addition to this, to have this ineffable being for our God, our portion, our all; to be permitted to say, This God is our God for ever and ever; to have his resplendent countenance smile upon us; to be encircled in his everlasting arms of power, and faithfulness, and love; to hear his voice saying to us, I am yours and you are mine; nothing shall ever pluck you from my hands, or separate you from my love, but you shall be with me where I am, behold my glory, and live to reign with me for ever and ever, this is too much; it is honor, it is glory, it is happiness too overwhelming, too transporting for mortal minds to conceive, or for mortal frames to support. O then, in all circumstances, under all inward and outward afflictions, let the children of Zion be joyful in their king.

You have, doubtless, often observed that when your minds have been intently and pleasingly occupied, you have become almost unconscious of the flight of time; minutes and hours have flown away with apparently unusual swiftness, and the setting or rising sun has surprised you, long before you expected its approach. But in heaven, the saints will be entirely lost and swallowed up in God; and their minds will be so completely absorbed in the contemplation of his ineffable, infinite, uncreated glories, that they will be totally unconscious how time, or rather, how eternity passes; and not only years, but millions of ages, such as we call ages, will be flown ere they are aware. Thus, a thousand years will seem to them but as one day, and yet so great, so ecstatic will be their happiness, that one day will be as a thousand years. And as there will be nothing to interrupt them, no bodily wants to call off their attention, no weariness to compel them to rest, no vicissitude of seasons, or of day and night, to disturb their contemplations: it is more than possible that innumerable ages may pass away, before they think of asking how long they have been in heaven, or even before they are conscious that a single hour has elapsed.

How often, Christians, have your hearts been made to burn with love, and gratitude, and admiration, and joy, whilst Christ has opened to you the scriptures, and caused you to know a little of that love whicn passeth knowledge! How often has one transient glimpse of the light of God's countenance turned your night into day, banished your sorrows, supported you under heavy afflictions, and caused you to rejoice with joy unspeakable and full of glory!   Oh, then, what must it be to escape for ever from error, ignorance, and darkness, and sin, into the region of bright, unclouded, eternal day; to see your God and Redeemer face to face; continually to contemplate, with immortal strength, glories so dazzlingly bright, that one moment's view of them would now, like a stream of lightning, turn your frail bodies into dust; to see the eternal volume of the divine counsels, the mighty map of the divine mind, unfolded to your eager, piercing gaze; to explore the heights and depths, the lengths and breadths of the Redeemer's love, and still to see new wonders, glories, and beauties, pouring upon your minds, in constant, endless succession, calling forth new songs of praise;—songs in which you will unite, not, as now, with mortal companions and mortal voices, but with the innumerable choir of angels, with the countless myriads of the redeemed, all shouting with a voice like the voice of many waters, Alleluia, for the Lord God omnipotent reigneth!— *Payson.*

'THOSE visions that the saved in heaven shall have of the love of Christ will far transcend our utmost knowledge here, even as far as the light of the sun at noon goes beyond the light of a blinking candle at midnight.—*Bunyan.*

WONDERS OF PROVIDENCE.

I HAVE no knowledge to take up the Lord in all his strange ways and passages of deep and unsearchable providences: for the Lord is before me, and I am so bemisted, that I cannot follow him; he is behind me, and I am not aware of him; he is above me, but his glory so dazzles my twilight of knowledge, that I cannot look up to him; he is upon my right hand, and I see him not; he is upon my left hand, and within me, and goeth and cometh, and his going and coming are a dream to me; he is round about me, and compasseth all my goings, and still I have him to seek. He is every way higher, and deeper, and broader, than the shallow and ebb hand-breadth of my short and dim light can take up; and therefore I would my heart could be silent, and sit down in the learnedly-ignorant wondering at that Lord, whom men and angels cannot comprehend. I know the highest angels who see him face to face, see not the borders of his infiniteness. And therefore it is my happiness to look afar off, and to light my dark candle at his brightness, and to have leave to sit and content myself with a traveller's light, without the clear vision of an enjoyer.—*Rutherford.*

It is hard work to believe, when the course of providence goeth cross-ways to our faith, and when misted souls in a dark night cannot know east by west, and our sea-compass seemeth to fail us. Every man is a believer in daylight: a fair day seemeth to be made all of faith and hope.—*Rutherford.*

Persecutions are beneficial to the righteous. They are a hail of precious stones, which, it is true, rob the vine of her leaves, but give her possessor a more precious treasure instead.—*Gossner.*

If ever I reach heaven, I expect to find three wonders there: first, to meet some I had not thought to see there; second, to meet some whom I had expected to miss there; but third,

the greatest wonder of all will be, to find *myself*
there !—*Dr. Watts.*

YOUTH AND AGE.

The seas are quiet when the winds are o'er ;—
So calm are we when passions are no more !
For then we know how vain it was to boast
Of fleeting things, so certain to be lost.

Clouds of affection from our younger eyes
Conceal that emptiness which age descries;
The soul's dark cottage, battered and decayed,
Lets in new light through chinks that time has made.

Stronger by weakness, wiser, men become,
As they draw near to their celestial home;
Leaving the old, both worlds at once they view
That stand upon the threshold of the new.—*Waller.*

CHEERFULNESS.

Cheerfulness and a festival spirit fill the soul
full of harmony ; it composes music for churches
and hearts ; it makes and publishes glorifications
of God ; it produces thankfulness, and serves the
end of charity ; and when the oil of gladness
runs over, it makes bright and tall emissions of
light and holy fires, reaching up to a cloud, and

making joy round about: and, therefore, since it is so innocent, and may be so pious and full of holy advantage, whatsoever can innocently minister to this holy joy, does set forward the work of religion and charity.—*Jeremy Taylor.*

PLEASURES OF SONG.

I LOVE to sing when I am glad,—
  Song is the echo of my gladness:
I long to sing when I am sad,
  Till song makes sweet my very sadness:
'Tis pleasant time when voices chime
  To some sweet rhyme in concert only;
And song to me is company,
  Good company, when I am lonely.

Whene'er I greet the morning light,
  My song goes forth in thankful numbers;
And, 'mid the shadows of the night,
  I sing me to my welcome slumbers:
My heart is stirred by each glad bird,
  Whose notes are heard in summer's bowers;
And song gives birth to friendly mirth,
  Around the hearth in wintry hours.

Man first learned song in Paradise,
  From the bright angels o'er him singing;
And in our home above the skies,
  Glad anthems are for ever ringing:

God lends his ear, well pleased to hear
　The songs that cheer his children's sorrow;
Till day shall break, and we shall wake
　Where love will make unfading morrow.

Then let me sing, while yet I may,
　Like him God loved, the sweet-toned Psalmist,
Who found in harp and holy lay
　The charm that keeps the spirit calmest:
For sadly here I need the cheer,
　While sinful fear with promise blendeth;
Oh! how I long to join the throng,
　Who sing the song that never endeth!—*Bethune.*

BEHOLDING GOD.—As, to a man who looks for a long time at the sun, the sun impresses itself upon everything; so is it with the man who looks much at God.—*Tauler.*

SPIRITUAL AFFECTIONS.

WHERE affections are spiritually renewed, the person of Christ is the centre of them. He is the spring, by his Spirit, that gives them life, light, and being; and he is the ocean that receives all their streams. God, even the Father, presents not himself in his beauty and amiableness as the object of our affections but as he is in Christ, acting his love in him. And as to all other spiritual things, renewed affections cleave to them according as they derive from Christ and lead to him; for he is to them all and in all. It is he whom the souls of his saints love for himself, for his own sake, and all other things in religion in and for him.

The air is pleasant and useful, that without which we cannot live or breathe; but if the sun did not enlighten it, and warm it with his beams: if it were always one perpetual night and cold, what refreshment could· be received by it? Christ is the sun of righteousness, and it his beams did not quicken, animate, and enlighten the best, the most necessary duties of religion, nothing desirable would remain in them. This is the most certain character of affections spiritually renewed. They can rest in nothing but in Christ; they fix on nothing but what is amiable by a participation of his beauty; and in whatever he is, therein they find complacency.—*Dr. Owen.*

AGED SINNER.—If we see a man in his old age grow more in love with the things of this woıld, and less in love with the things of God, it is not through the weakness of nature, but through the strength of sin.—*Dr. Owen.*

THE PROGRESS OF GRACE IN THE SOUL.

THE believer's feelings and experience in the different stages of the divine life are essentially and necessarily different. There is a dawning brightness, a vernal glow of freshness about the early days of grace, which must pass away, and can never be recalled again. This is not to be confounded with backsliding or declension in grace. The blade of spring, indeed, gradually loses its freshness, and its verdant loveliness passes away; but it is ripening, not withering; and lovely as the budding verdure of spring is, the mellow glow of autumn is lovelier. So it is with ripening as compared with early grace. Its impressions are less vivid, but they are more deep and abiding. Its feelings are less ardent, but they are calmer and holier. Its peace may not so overflow, but it ploughs a deeper channel. It is not so exulting and sanguine, but it is more solemn, more chastened, more lowly. There is less of the flesh, more of the spirit—less excitement, more grace. John, when now laden with years and labors he was carried into the congregation, and could only look round and smile, and say, " Little children, love one another," must have been much changed in feeling from what he was, when in the fire of his first love, he obtained the name of a "son of thunder ;" and yet he was far liker Jesus, and far nearer glory. Therefore, beloved, be not cast down. Though feelings change, though comforts decline, though there be ups and downs, clouds and storms, as you travel on, still be of good courage, and hold on your way. Rather rejoice, and bless the Lord that he that began the good work is carrying it on,—that the long year of grace is gradually running its course ; that the spring is already over, that the summer is pressing on, and that amid changing suns and showers, storms and calms, you are ripening for the eternal harvest. Only seek to be holier, daily nearer the Lord, daily more like Jesus, and then all is well. Soon shall time give place to eternity. Soon shall sin, and sorrow, and change, end for ever. Soon shall the day break, and the shadows flee away.—*Islay Burns.*

CHRISTIAN EXPERIENCE.

AT first, in the early days of fresh experience and warm first love, the believer shoots up like the palm-tree, and in a little time seems almost ripe for glory. His joyful steps, "like hinds'-feet," carry him swiftly on, and before he has almost entered on the heavenly pilgrimage, he seems already on the very confines of Canaan. He breathes after heaven. He longs to be with Jesus. Heaven, though still future, seems already begun within him. His peace is as a river, his joy unspeakable and full of glory. The fountain of life eternal gushes up within his heart. It is a very Beulah of holy peace, and love, and gladness, and the breezes of heaven are around him. He is already *almost* in glory! Then he fondly dreams—but, alas! it is but a dream. He is yet far from home. He is not " meet for the inheritance of the saints in light." His experience, joyful and blessed as it. is, is yet superficial, in many points deceitful and unreal. His faith, though ardent and sanguine, is as yet little tried. His joy, so exulting and so full, is yet sadly mixed up with presumption and vain fleshly feeling. His love, though warm, is selfish—joying in the

Lord for his gifts, rather than for himself. The old man is yet strong within him. There are unfathomed depths of corruption within, of which he knows nothing. Self, that oldest and foulest idol, still lurks within, and has scarce as yet got one deadly wound. He has thus much to learn, much to suffer, and much to do, before he can overcome and be crowned. Hence he must go back to the wilderness again, and, like the redeemed flock in every age, pass " through great tribulations "—that, being refined by the furnace, and moulded and fashioned under Jehovah's hand as a vessel of mercy, he may be found at last unto praise, and honor, and glory, at the appearing of Jesus Christ.—*Islay Burns.*

DEATH A BLESSING TO THE AGED SAINT.

The chief benefit of our age is, our near approach to our journey's end ; for the end of all motion is rest : which when we have once attained, there is nothing but fruition.

Now our age brings us, after a weary race, within some breathings of our goal : for if young men may die, old men must ; a condition which a mere carnal heart bewails, envying the oaks which many generations of men must leave standing and growing.

No marvel: for the worldling thinks himself here at home, and looks upon death as a banish-ment: he hath placed his heaven here below, and can see nothing in his remove, but either annihilation or torment.

But for us Christians, who know that while we are present in the body we are absent from the Lord, and account ourselves foreigners, our life a pilgrimage, heaven our home, how can we but rejoice, that after a tedious and painful travel, we now draw near to the threshold of our Father's house, wherein we know there are many mansions, and all glorious? I could blush to hear a heathen say, " If God would offer me the choice of renewing my age, and returning to my first childhood, I should heartily refuse it; for I should be loth, after I have passed so much of my race, to be called back from the goal to the bars of my first setting out ;" and to hear a Christian whining at the thought of his dissolu-tion ! Where is our faith of a heaven, if, having been so long sea-beaten, we are loth to think of putting into the safe and blessed harbor of im-mortality ?—*Bishop Hall.*

FRAILTY OF AGE.—It is as natural for old age to be frail, as for the stalk to bend under the ripened ear, or for the autumnal leaf to change its hue.—*Blair*.

CHRIST'S SPIRIT OF FORGIVENESS.

WHEN on the fragrant sandal-tree
  The woodman's axe descends,
And she, who bloomed so beauteously,
  Beneath the keen stroke bends,
E'en on the edge that wrought her death,
Dying she breathes her sweetest breath,
As if betokening in her fall
Peace to her foes and love to all.
How hardly man this lesson learns,
To smile, and bless the hand that spurns;
To see the blow, to feel the pain,
But render only love again !
This spirit not to earth is given ;
One had it, but He came from heaven.
Reviled, rejected, and betrayed,
No curse he breathed, no plaint he made ;
But when in death's deep pang he sighed,
Prayed for his murderers, and died.—*Anon*.

DEATH A SLEEP.

THOU art afraid of death :—when thou art weary of thy day's labor, art thou afraid of rest ?

Hear what thy Saviour, who is the Lord of life, esteems of death :—" Our friend Lazarus sleepeth."

So, the philosophers of old were wont to call sleep the brother of death : but God says, death is no other than sleep itself: a sleep both sure and sweet. When thou liest down at night to thy repose, thou canst not be so certain to awake again in the morning, as, when thou layest thyself down in death, thou art sure to awake in the morning of the resurrection. Out of this bodily sleep thou mayest be startled with fearful dreams, with tumults, or alarms of war ; but here, thou shalt rest quietly in the place of silence, free from all inward and outward disturbances : while, in the meantime, thy soul shall see none but visions of joy and blessedness.

But, oh the sweet and heavenly expression of our last rest, and the issue of our happy resuscitation ! " For if we believe that Jesus died and rose again, even so them also which sleep in Jesus, will God bring with him." So, our belief is antidote enough against the worst of death. And why are we troubled with death, when we believe that Jesus died ? and what a triumph is this over death, that the same Jesus who died rose again! and what a comfort it is, that the same Jesus who arose shrall both come again, and bring all his with him in glory! and, lastly, what a strong cordial is this to all good hearts, that all those who die well do sleep in Jesus! Thou thoughtest, perhaps, of sleeping in the bed of the grave, and there, indeed, is rest; but he tells thee of sleeping in the bosom of Jesus, and there is immortality and blessedness.—*Bishop Hall.*

BENEFIT OF TRIALS.

If the Lord is pleased to sanctify the infirmities to which our present mortal frame is subject, we shall have cause to praise him at last, no less for the bitter than ·the sweet. I am convinced in my judgment, that a cross or a pinch somewhere or other, is so necessary to us, that we cannot go on well for a considerable time without one. We live on an enchanted ground, are surrounded with snares, and if not quickened by trials, are very prone to sink into formality or carelessness. It is a shame it should be so, but so it is, that a long course of prosperity always makes us drowsy. Trials, therefore, are medicines, which our gracious and wise physician prescribes because we need them; and he proportions the frequency and weight of them to what the case requires. Many of his people are sharply exercised by poverty, which is a continual trial every day, and all the year round. Others have trials in their families. They who have comfortable firesides, and a competence for this world, often suffer by sickness, either in their own persons, or in the persons of those they love But any or all of these crosses are mercies, if the Lord works by them to prevent us from cleaving to the world, from backsliding in heart or life, and to keep us nearer to himself. Let us trust our Physician and he will surely do us good. . And let us thank him for all his prescriptions, for without them our soul-sickness would quickly grow upon us.—*John Newton.*

If we saw our Father's house, and that great and fair city, the New Jerusalem, which is up above sun and moon, we would cry to be over the water, and to be carried in Christ's arms out of this borrowed prison.—*Rutherford.*

The Christian's Hope.—Time flies apace, and past troubles will return no more: every pulse we feel beats a sharp moment of the pain away, and the *last* stroke will come. Then sorrow and sighing shall flee away, and joy and gladness shall come forth to conduct us home.— *John Newton.*

COMPLETE IN CHRIST.

O how sweet to be wholly Christ's, and wholly in Christ! to be out of the creature's owning, and made complete in Christ, to live by faith in Christ; and to be once for all clothed with the created majesty and glory of the Son of God, wherein he makes all his friends and followers sharers! to dwell in Immanuel's high and blessed land, and live in that sweetest air, where no wind bloweth, but the breathings of the Holy Ghost: no seas nor floods flow, but the pure waters of life, that proceed from under the throne, and from the Lamb: no planting, but the tree of life that yieldeth twelve manner of fruit every month! What do we here but sin and suffer? O when shall the nights be gone, the shadows flee away, and the morning of that long, long day, without cloud or night, dawn! The Spirit and the bride say, Come; O when shall the Lamb's wife be ready, and the Bridegroom say, Come!—*Rutherford.*

FEAR OF DEATH.

THOU fearest death: thou wert not a man, if thou didst not so: the holiest, the wisest, the strongest, that ever were, have done no less. He is the king of fear, and therefore may and must command it. Thou mayest hear the man after God's own heart say, "The sorrows of death compassed me; my soul is full of troubles, my life draweth nigh to the grave." Thou mayest hear great and good Hezekiah, upon the message of his death, chattering like a crane or a swallow, and mourning as a dove.

Thou fearest as a man: I cannot blame thee: but thou must overcome thy fear, as a Christian, which thou shalt do, if, from the terrible aspect of the messenger, thou shalt cast thine eyes upon the gracious and amiable face of the God that sends him. "Lo, our God is the God of salvation; and unto God the Lord belong the issues of death." Make him thy friend, and death shall be no other than advantage. Precious in the sight of the Lord is the death of his saints.— *Bishop Hall.*

DEATH A BLESSING TO THE CHRISTIAN.

" BETTER is the day of death than the day of one's birth." Better, every way. Our birth begins our miseries; our death ends them : our birth enters the best of men into a wretched world; our death enters the good into a world of glory. Certainly, were it not for our unbelief, as we came crying into the world, so we should go singing out of it. And if some have solemnized their birth-day with feasting and triumph, the church of old hath bestowed that name and cost upon the death's day of her martyrs and saints.—*Bishop Hall.*

DEATH VANQUISHED.

THE power of death, the last enemy, is destroyed, as it respects all who believe in Christ. Instead of being the jailor of hell and the grave, he is now, as it respects Christ's people, the porter of Paradise. All he can now do is to cause them to sleep in Jesus, release their immortal spirits from the fetters which bind them to earth, and deposit their weary bodies in the tomb as a place of rest, till Christ comes at the last day, to raise them incorruptible, glorious, and immortal, and re-unite them to their souls in a state of perfect, never-ending felicity.—*Payson.*

THE HOPE OF THE CHRISTIAN.

When the heathen Socrates was to die for his religion, he comforted himself with this, that he should go to the place where he should see Orpheus, Homer, Musæus, and the worthies of the former ages. Poor man! could he have come to have known God manifested in the flesh, and received up into glory, and there, in that glorified flesh, sitting at the right hand of Majesty; could he have attained to know the blessed order of the cherubim and seraphim, angels, archangels, principalities, and powers, and the rest of the most glorious hierarchy of heaven; could he have been acquainted with that celestial choir of the spirits of just men made perfect; could he have reached to know the God and Father of spirits, the infinitely and incomprehensibly glorious

Deity, whose presence transfuses everlasting blessedness into all those citizens of glory; and could he have known that he should have an undoubted interest instantly upon his dissolution, in that infinite bliss; how much more gladly would he have taken off his hemlock, and how much more joyfully would he have passed into that happier world !—*Bishop Hall.*

DEATH OF JOHN BUNYAN.

HE comforted those that wept about him, exhorting them to trust in God, and pray to him for mercy and forgiveness of their sins, telling them what a glorious exchange it would be to leave their troubles and cares of a wretched mortality to live with Christ for ever, with peace and joy inexpressible; expounding to them the comfortable scriptures by which they were to hope and assuredly come unto a blessed resurrection in the last day.   He desired some to pray with him, and he joined with them in prayer, and his last words, after he had struggled with a languishing disease, were these, " Weep not for me, but for yourselves : I go to the Father of our Lord Jesus Christ, who will, through the mediation of his blessed Son, receive me though a sinner, where I hope we ere long shall meet to sing the new song, and remain everlastingly happy, world without end."—*From the earliest Biography of Bunyan.*

SONG OF DEATH.

SHRINK not, O Human Spirit,
The Everlasting arm is strong to save!
Look up, look up, frail Nature, put thy trust
In Him who went down mourning to the dust,
And overcame the grave!
Quickly goes down the sun;
Life's work is almost done;
Fruitless endeavor, hope deferred, and strife!
One little struggle more,
One pang, and then is o'er
All the long, mournful weariness of life.
Kind friends, 'tis almost past,
Come now and look your last!
Sweet children, gather near,
And his last blessing hear,
See how he loved you who departeth now!
And with thy trembling step and pallid brow
O, most beloved one,
Whose breast he leaned upon,
Come, faithful unto death,
.Receive his parting breath.

The fluttering spirit panteth to be free,
Hold him not back who speeds to victory ;
The bonds are riven, the struggling soul is free !

Hail, hail, enfranchised spirit !
Thou that the wine-press of the field hast trod !
On, blest immortal, on, through boundless space,
And stand with thy Redeemer face to face ;
And stand before thy God !
Life's weary work is o'er,
Thou art of earth no more :
No more art trammelled by the oppressive clay,
But tread'st with winged ease
The high acclivities
Of truths sublime, up Heaven's crystalline way.
Here no bootless guest ;
The city's name is Rest ;
Here shall no fear appal ;
Here love is all in all ;
Here shalt thou win thy ardent soul's desire ;
Here clothe thee in thy beautiful attire.
Lift, lift thy wondering eyes !
Yonder is Paradise,
And this fair, shining band
Are spirits of thy land !
And these that throng to meet thee are thy kin,
Who have awaited thee, redeemed from sin !
The city's gates unfold—enter, oh ! enter in !

Household Words.

DEATH OF STANDFAST.

WHEN Mr. Standfast had thus set things in order, and the time being come for him to haste him away, he went down to the river. Now there was a great calm at that time in the river; wherefore Mr. Standfast, when he was about half way in, stood a while and talked to his companions that had waited upon him thither; and he said, " This river has been a terror to many: yea, the thoughts of it also have often frightened me! now, methinks, I stand easy; my foot is fixed upon that on which the feet of the priests that bore the ark of the covenant stood, while Israel went over this Jordan. The waters indeed are to the palate bitter, and to the stomach cold; yet the thoughts of what I am going to, and of the convoy that waits for me on the other side, do lie as a glowing coal at my heart. I see myself now at the end of my journey; my toilsome days are ended. I am going to see that head that was crowned with thorns, and that face that was spit upon for me. I have formerly lived by hearsay and faith, but now I go where I shall live by sight, and shall be with him in whose company I delight myself. I have loved to hear my Lord spoken of; and wherever I have seen the print of his shoe in the earth, there I have coveted to set my foot too. His name has been to me as a civet-box, yea sweeter than all perfumes. His voice to me has been most sweet, and his countenance I have more desired than they that have most desired the light of the sun. His words I did use to gather for my food, and for antidotes against my faintings. He hath held me, and hath kept me from mine iniquities; yea, my steps have been strengthened in his way."

Now while he was thus in discourse, his countenance changed, his " strong man bowed under him," and after he had said, " Take me, for I am come unto Thee," he ceased to be seen of them.

But glorious it was to see how the open region was filled with horses and chariots, with trumpeters and pipers, with singers and players on stringed instruments, to welcome the pilgrims as they went up and followed one another in at the beautiful gate of the city.—*Bunyan.*

DEATH is the dropping of the flower, that the fruit may swell.—*H. W. Beecher.*

LONELINESS.

In the hearts of the aged a feeling of loneliness is apt to dwell,—often as an invited and cherished guest. They seem to stand alone, having few interests or sympathies in common with those around them. Their day, they think, is over; their labor past, their influence gone, it only remains that they await, as patiently as may be, the day of their death. While the young have their congenial circle, and manhood its thronged sphere of activity, they, the aged, must dwell apart and alone, already neglected and forgotten, save that here and there lingers yet o solitary companion, like themselves, strangers in the earth. They live in the memory of departed scenes, snatching a brief pleasure from the retrospect, oftener a lengthened sorrow. They revisit the fountains where their childhood had drank many a cup of pleasure ; but, as they linger, the fountains cease to flow—they turn away to weep. And those who there had quaffed with them the exhilarating draught, where are they ? Long ago the silver cord was loosed, and the golden bowl broken at the cistern. What is there now to live for ?

Into this hidden sanctuary of grief we would not intrude with words of harsh reproof. It is not without cause that the aged often yield to melancholy broodings. They have seen one and another of their companions fall around them, until few remain. They are conscious of gathering infirmities; they cannot mingle as once in the gay or the rough scenes of life. The gallant ship, which had rode out many a storm, and carried many a precious freight, is now drawn up into the harbor, to engage no more in the strifes of the elements.

But may not this feeling of isolation be in no small degree morbid and mistaken? Often the aged have more and warmer friends than they are willing to believe. Often their opinions are respected where they imagine themselves altogether without influence. Often they have a mission to perform, less active, it may be, but no less real and blessed, than when their energies were at the full. Would they only place themselves in closer sympathy with the younger generation, and bring forth the ripened fruits of their long experience, they would find themselves welcomed where they now feel that they are a burden. When wisdom falls kindly from aged lips, it makes its way to the heart.

But, at the worst as to earthly society, the true disciples of Christ have in him a friend ever at hand, who sticketh closer than a brother ; whose love knows no change, no abatement. Faith, which he most earnestly invites them to exercise, can surround them with his perpetual presence. They cannot be alone. He is more than sons and daughters, more than all the loved ones that are gone. He was of old even from everlasting, yet upon him rests the dew of youth. He ever liveth a personal Friend. He is touched with the feeling of your infirmities, aged believers. Others may desert, but he remains true ; others may die, but he lives. And, besides, your aged friends who have slept in Jesus are still in him. You and they are in him. The sacred bond is unbroken. Absent in body, they are still with you in him. Earth and heaven are blended. On this ladder which Jacob saw, they who are gone may still come down to be with you. Soon you shall mount up. and then you shall see them face to face.

THE VALE OF TEARS.

O, CHILD of grief, remember the vale of tears is much frequented; thou art not alone in thy distress. Sorrow has a numerous family. Say not I am *the* man that hath seen affliction, for there be others in the furnace with thee. Remember, moreover, the King of kings once went through this valley, and here he obtained his name, " the man of sorrows ; " for it was while passing through it he became " acquainted with grief."—*Spurgeon.*

CHRIST A GUEST.

IF thou desirest Christ for a perpetual guest, give him all the keys of thine heart; let not one cabinet be locked up from him; give him the range of every room, and the key of every chamber ; thus you will constrain him to remain. —*Spurgeon.*

THE CHRISTIAN'S THOUGHTS OF DEATH.

As I grow older and come nearer to death, I look upon it more and more with complacent joy; and out of every longing I hear God say, " O, thirsting, hungering one, come to me ! What the

other life will bring I know not, only that I shall
awake in God's likeness, and see him as he is.

Beat on, then, O heart, and yearn for dying !
I have drank at many a fountain, but thirst came
again ; I have fed at many a bounteous table,
but hunger returned ; I have seen many bright
and lovely things, but while I gazed their lustre
faded.   There is nothing here that can give me
rest ; but when I behold thee, O God, I shall be
satisfied.—*H. W. Beecher.*

FAITH.

Alas ! it is the slowest and most painful lesson that Faith has to learn,—Faith, not Indifference,—to do steadfastly and patiently all that
lies to her hand, and there leave it, believing
that the Almighty is able to govern his own
world.

SOLITUDE.

There is a solitude which old age feels to be
as natural and satisfying as that rest which
seems such an irksomeness to youth, but which
gradually grows into the best blessing of our
lives.   And there is another solitude so full of

11*

peace and hope that it is like Jacob's sleep in the wilderness, at the foot of the ladder of angels.—*Chambers' Journal.*

BLESSED ARE THEY THAT MOURN.

O, DEEM not they are blest alone,
  Whose lives a peaceful tenor keep;
For God, who pities man, has shown
  A blessing for the eyes that weep.

The light of smiles shall fill again
  The lids that overflow with tears;
And weary hours of woe and pain
  Are promises of happier years.

There is a day of sunny rest
  For every dark and troubled night;
And grief may bide an evening guest,
  But joy shall come with early light.

Nor let the good man's trust depart,
  Though life its common gifts deny;
Though, with a pierced and broken heart,
  And spurned of men, he goes to die.

For God has marked each sorrowing day,
  And numbered every secret tear,
And heaven's long age of bliss shall pay
  For all his children suffer here.

BRYANT.

EXCELLENCY OF CHRIST.

CHRIST is a flower, but he fadeth not; he is a river, but he is never dry; he is a sun, but he knoweth no eclipse; he is all in all, but he is something more than all.—*Spurgeon.*

NOT THE ONLY MOURNER.

O, MOURNER, say not that *thou* art a target for all the arrows of the Almighty; take not to thyself the preëminence of woe: for thy fellows have trodden the valley too, and upon them are the scars of the thorns and briers of the dreary pathway.—*Spurgeon.*

A BEAUTIFUL OLD AGE.

BEAUTIFUL to behold is the old man whose heart still beats in warm sympathy with the generation from which he is passing away. His setting sun casts its mild radiance over the world that he is leaving. He would not wrap himself in clouds, as if in haste to withdraw his light, but would still shine on in gladness, as long as he lingers above the horizon. When he departs, he still lives on earth in the soft twilight of his blessed memory.

He is an old man; he has passed through many trials, he has experienced the treachery of false friends; but his heart is more tender than in his youth, his sympathies are deeper and broader. He does not withdraw within the narrow circle of self, to brood over real or fancied slights; he does not perpetually disparage the present in contrast with the past; he does not turn scornfully away from everything new, as necessarily evil. He has turned his knowledge of the world to better account. Without the enthusiasm of his younger days, he is still hopeful, but with a wise sobriety gained in a long and varied experience, wherein he has learned to distinguish between the seeming and the real, the ephemeral and the permanent. Thus he is fitted to be a wise counsellor, speaking the truth in love. Even his reproofs, so kindly uttered, are received with a feeling deeper than respect. The children flee not at his approach, for they know he has a pleasant word for them; and when he changes his tone from gay to grave, and points to a loving Saviour, or to brighter worlds, they linger gladly in his presence. He is welcome everywhere. His hoary head is a crown of glory. Blessed old man, he has been with Jesus. The love of Christ constrains him. He shall not die unwept.

I'M GROWING OLD.

I 'M growing old—'t is surely so;
   And yet how short it seems
Since I was but a sportive child,
   Enjoying childish dreams!

I cannot *see* the change that comes
   With such an even pace;
I mark not when the wrinkles fall
   Upon my fading face.

I know I 'm old; and yet my heart
   Is just as young and gay
As e'er it was before my locks
   Of bright brown turned to gray.

I know these eyes to other eyes
   Look not so bright and glad
As once they looked; and yet 't is not
   Because my heart 's more sad.

I never watched with purer joy
   The floating clouds and glowing skies,
While glistening tears of rapture fill
   These old and fading eyes.

And when I mark the cheek where once
  The bright rose used to glow,
It grieves me not to see instead
  The almond crown my brow.

I 've seen the flower grow old and pale,
  And withered more than I ;
I 've seen it lose its every charm,
  Then droop away and die.

And then I 've seen it rise again,
  Bright as the beaming sky,
And young and pure and beautiful—
  And felt that so shall I.

Then what if I *am* growing old ?—
  My heart is changeless still,
And God has given me enough
  This loving heart to fill.

I love to see the sun go down,
  And lengthening shadows throw
Along the ground, while o'er my head
  The clouds in crimson glow.

I see, beyond those gorgeous clouds,
  A country bright and fair,
Which needs no sun : God and the Lamb
  Its light and beauty are.

I seem to hear the wondrous song
  ,Redeemed sinners sing ;

And my heart leaps to join the throng
　　To praise the Heavenly King.

I seem to see three cherub boys,
　　As hand in hand they go,
With golden curls and snowy wings,
　　Whose eyes with rapture glow.

When I was young I called them mine—
　　Now Heaven's sweet ones are they;
But I shall claim my own again,
　　When I am called away.

Perhaps, when heaven's bright gate I 've passed,
　　They 'll know from every other
The one who gave them back to God,
　　And haste to call me mother.

O! I am glad I 'm growing old!
　　For every day I spend
Shall bring me one day nearer that
　　Bright day that has no end.

OLD AGE.

THE neglected portion of the great American family is old age—we are sorry to say. Not that we, as a nation, are disrespectful to the old, or that they are denied or grudged anything. We perform the *negative* duty to them, by avoid ing all which shall occasion to them offence or deprivation ; but we do not perform the positive duty of assiduously seeing that they occupy, always and only, the places of honor and prominence ; nor more particularly do we study to contrive, untiringly and affectionately, how to comfort, strengthen, cheer, and recuperate them. The old man in one house may have his chair in the drawing-room, and his place at the table, and be listened to when he speaks, and obeyed when he commands. But in another house he will have his easy-chair cushioned and pillowed, and his arm-chair at the table, and the cook will be busied most with what will newly nourish or refresh his more delicate appetite ; while all listen first for his words, and address conversation to him as a centre, and eagerly seek for his commands as an authority. This (we assure the reader, from our own well-weighed observation in both countries) is a fair picture of the difference between old age in America and old age in England.

It is an unconscious fault in our country— an oversight of our life too busy, our attention too overtasked, and our plans of home and pleasure too unsettled and immature; but the feeling for better things is in us, and time will bring this feeling into action.—*N. P. Willis.*

THE best and most polished nations of antiquity held the aged in high honor. Those of the same character among the moderns will find their highest good, as well as purest pleasure, in imitating their example. A tender sapling of the forest is doubtless an object of interest to every man of heart or taste; but the oak that has braved a century of years cannot be passed by any being, but a savage, without strong emotion and profound veneration.—*Newark Daily Advertiser.*

HOW TO BE HAPPIER.

SAID a venerable farmer, some eighty years of age, to a relative who visited him, "I have lived on this farm for more than half a century. I have no desire to change my residence as long as I live on earth. I have no desire to be richer than I now am. I have worshipped the God of my fathers with the same people for more than forty years. During that period I have been rarely absent from the sanctuary on the Sabbath, and have never lost but one communion season. I have never been confined to my bed by sickness a single day. The blessings of life have been richly spread around me, and I made up my mind, long ago, that if I wished to become happier, *I must have more religion.*"

HERE thou art but a stranger, travelling to thy country, where the glories of a kingdom are prepared for thee ; it is, therefore, a huge folly to be much afflicted because thou hast a less convenient inn to lodge in by the way.

GROWING OLD.

To "grow old gracefully," is a good and beautiful thing ; to grow old worthily, a better. And the first effort to that end is not only to recognize, but to become personally reconciled to, the fact of youth's departure ; to see, or, if not seeing, to have faith in, the wisdom of that which we call change, yet which is in truth progression ; to follow, openly and fearlessly, in ourselves and our own life, the same law which makes spring pass into summer, summer into autumn, autumn into winter, preserving an especial beauty and fitness in each of the four.

Yes, if women could only believe it, there is a wonderful beauty even in growing old. The charm of expression arising from softened temper or ripened intellect often amply atones for the loss of form and coloring ; and, consequently, to those who never could boast either of these latter, years give much more than they take away. Many a one, who was absolutely plain in youth, thus grows pleasant and well-looking in declining years.—*Chambers' Journal.*

CHRIST THE FOUNDATION.

MEN who build on any other foundation than the rock Christ Jesus are like birds that build in trees by the side of rivers. The bird sings in the branches, and the river sings below, but all the while the waters are undermining the soil about the roots, till, in some unsuspected hour, the tree falls with a crash into the stream ; and then its nest is sunk, its home is gone, and the bird is a wanderer. But birds that hide their young in the clefts of the rock are undisturbed, and, after every winter, coming again, they find their nests awaiting them, and all their life long brood the summer in the same places, impregnable to time or storm.—*H. W. Beecher.*

PEACE IN GOD.

"Let my soul calm itself in Thee ; I say, let the great sea of my soul, that swelleth with waves, calm itself in Thee."—*St. Augustine.*

Life's mystery—deep, restless as the ocean—
   Hath surged and wailed for ages to and fro;
Earth's generations watch in ceaseless motion,
   As in and out its hollow moanings flow ;
Shivering and yearning by that unknown sea,
Let my soul calm itself, O Christ, in thee !

Life's sorrows, with inexorable power,
   Sweep desolation o'er this mortal plain ;
And human loves and hopes fly as the chaff
   Borne by the whirlwind from the ripened grain.
Ah, when before that blast my hopes all flee,
Let my soul calm itself, O Christ, in thee !

Between the mysteries of death and life
   Thou standest, loving, guiding—not explaining ;
We ask, and thou art silent—yet we gaze,
   And our charmed hearts forget their drear complaining !
No crushing fate, no stony destiny !
Thou Lamb that hast been slain, we rest in thee ! ·

The many waves of thought, the mighty tides,
  The ground-swell that rolls up from other lands,
From far-off worlds, from dim eternal shores,
  Whose echo dashes on life's wave-worn strands,—
This vague, dark tumult of the inner sea
Grows calm, grows bright, O risen Lord, in thee!

Thy pierced hand guides the mysterious wheels;
  Thy thorn-crowned brow now wears the crown of power;
And when the dark enigma presseth sore,
  Thy patient voice saith, " Watch with ME one hour!"
As sinks the moaning river in the sea
In silver peace, so sinks my soul in thee!

H. B. Stowe.

EVERY MAN'S LIFE A PLAN OF GOD.

EVERY human soul has a complete and perfect plan cherished for it in the heart of God—a divine biography marked out, which it enters into life, to live. This life, rightfully unfolded, will be a complete and beautiful whole; an experience led on by God, and unfolded by the secret nurture of the world; a drama cast in the mould of a perfect art, with no part wanting; a divine study for the man himself, and for others; a study that shall forever unfold, in wondrous beauty, the love and faithfulness of God; great in its conception, great in the divine skill by which it is shaped; above all, great in the momentous and glorious issues it prepares. What a thought is this for every human soul to cherish! What dignity does it add to life! What support does it bring to the trials of life! What instigation does it add to send us on in everything that constitutes our excellence! We live in the divine thought. We fill a place in the great everlasting plan of God's intelligence. We never sink below his care, never drop out of his counsel.—*Dr. Bushnell.*

O LORD, take my heart, for I cannot give it; and when thou hast it, O keep it, for I cannot keep it for thee; and save me in spite of myself, for Jesus Christ's sake.—*Fenelon.*

KIND words are the brightest flowers of earth's existence; they make a very paradise of the humblest home the world can show. Use them, especially around the fireside circle. They are jewels beyond price, and more precious to heal the wounded heart, and make the weigheddown spirit glad, than all other blessings the earth can give.

TWO IN HEAVEN.

" You have two children," said I.

" I have four," was the reply ; " two on earth, two in heaven."

There spoke the mother ! Still hers, only gone before ! Still remembered, loved, and cherished, by the hearth and at the board ; their places not yet filled, even though their successors draw life from the same faithful breast where their dying heads were pillowed.

" Two in heaven ! "

Safely housed from storm and tempest. No sickness there, nor drooping head, nor fading eyes, nor weary feet. By the green pastures, tended by the Good Shepherd, linger the little lambs of the heavenly fold.

" Two in heaven ! "

Earth less attractive ; eternity nearer ; invisible cords drawing the maternal soul upwards. " Still, small voices " ever whisper " Come ! " to the world-weary spirit.

" Two in heaven ! "

Mother of angels, walk softly ! Holy eyes watch thy footsteps ;—cherub forms bend to listen ! Keep thy spirit free from earth-taint ; so shalt thou go to them, though they may not return to thee.

RECOGNITION IN HEAVEN.

I MUST confess, as the experience of my own soul, that the expectation of loving my friends in heaven principally kindles my love to them while on earth. If I thought I should never know them, and consequently never love them, after this life is ended, I should number them with temporal things, and love them as such ; but I now converse with my pious friends in a firm persuasion that I shall converse with them forever ; and I take comfort in those that are dead or absent, believing that I shall shortly meet them in heaven, and love them with a heavenly love.—*Baxter*.

THE OTHER SIDE.

ONCE, on the Thames, the boat in which Archbishop Leighton was with others came near going to the bottom. The rest were pale with terror, but he was perfectly calm. To some who expressed astonishment at his serenity and self-possession, he replied, " Why, what harm would it have been, if we had been safely landed on the *other side ?* "

DYING IN CHRIST.

THE graves are no longer silent, since the grave of Jesus is open. The tombstones upon which the cross stands press not heavily. In every burial-ground I hear the words, " I live, and ye shall live also."—*Tholuck.*

THE true Christian is always young.—*Schleiermacher.*

HEAVEN'S REVELATIONS.

THE entering into heaven will reveal many things unknown on earth. Some whom the world thought saint-like will barely gain admittance there ; and others, who went all their lives in doubt and dread, will have angelic welcome, and an abundant entrance into the heavenly kingdom. " The first shall be last, and the last shall be first."—*H. W. Beecher.*

MAN'S LIFE.

THE life of every man is as the well-spring of a stream, whose small beginnings are indeed plain to all, but whose ulterior course and destination, as it winds through the expanses of infinite years, only the Omniscient can discern. —*Carlyle.*

A WORLDLY OLD MAN.

THERE is not a more repulsive spectacle than an old man who will not forsake the world, which has already forsaken him.—*Tholuck.*

AGED SINNERS.

LIKE the worm clinging to the withered leaf, they feed upon the faded memories of departed days, which shall never return.—*Tholuck.*

OLD AGE.

OLD age, says the proverb, is a courtier; he knocks again and again at the window and at the door, and makes us everywhere conscious of his presence. Woe to the man who becomes old without becoming wise; woe to him if this world shuts the door without the future having opened its portals to him.—*Tholuck.*

THE DEATH OF MOSES.

Sweet was the journey to the sky
　The wondrous prophet tried;—
" Climb up the mount," said God, " and die!"
　The prophet climbed and died.

Softly his fainting head he lay
　Upon his Maker's breast;
His Maker kissed his soul away,
　And laid his flesh to rest.

In God's own arms he left the breath
　That God's own Spirit gave;
His was the noblest road to death,
　And his the sweetest grave.—*Watts.*

THAT DEAR OLD SOUL.

" That dear old soul!"　The very words
bring up vividly to the mind's eye one long since
gone to her rest, to whose name they were for
years a sweet appendage.　When first we saw
her, her hair was blanched by many winters and
many sorrows; but each of those winters had
been succeeded by a balmy spring, each sorrow
by a sanctified joy.　Never till then did age
seem beautiful.　I had regarded one advanced in
years like a tree in autumn, stripped of its
leaves, robbed of its fruit, and standing only for

the mad winds and the wild storms to whistle through and beat against.   But in " Mother Allen " I saw the leaves only nipt and faded,— the tree stood firm and strong, with its boughs still bending beneath their weight of golden fruit.

Her abundant hair was soft and silvery white, daubed with no vile dye, and hidden beneath no tress stolen from the brow of youth.   It was combed plainly over that calm, pure brow, which even time had not the power to wrinkle.   Beautiful she could never have been even in sunny girlhood, for her features were large and irregular ; but lovely she was, even to the eyes of strangers, who had yet to learn her worth.   Her eyes were deeply set, giving an earnest, thoughtful expression to her face, while the calm smile on her lips told of the perfect peace which dwelt in her bosom.   In her face one might have found a fulfilment of the promise, " He shall have perfect peace whose mind is stayed on Thee."

Mother Allen was no lady of leisure, with nothing to disturb her mind or interfere with her tranquillity.   In early life, while her children were with her, she was called to drink the cup of poverty and unrequited love, to the very dregs. Many an hour of anguish did she pass in comparing the happy days of her maidenhood with her then present cruel desolation. Many a night, while the tempest roared among the trees which surrounded her comfortless home, while he who had sworn to protect her was a wanderer in the haunts of vice, did she kneel beside her sleeping babes, and plead with her mother's God that He would shield the defenceless stranger and her darling little ones. How often, in solemn midnight, did her plaintive voice mingle with the murmuring of the pines, while she pleaded with Him who " heareth the young ravens when they cry," that He would send bread in the desert to those who were of more value than they! In her agony for her husband, she would sometimes almost forget the temporal wants of her family, and cry unto Him who came to seek the lost that He would restore the beloved, deluded wanderer, back to purity, to home, and to duty. And she brought her case before the throne as if she expected an answer of mercy. When the morning broke upon her sleepless eyes, she would gaze from the door of her unfinished dwelling on all the beauties God had spread out to cheer the heart of the weary. And for these she offered heartfelt praise. Some persons, when in anguish of spirit, almost reproach nature for its calm, joyous course. They feel as if it heightened their sorrow to see all things gay around them ; they feel that nature should cast off her mantle of green, and robe herself in sackcloth ; that the flowers should wither, the stars fade, the sun hide its face, and the birds change their warbles into wailing dirges, all because one soul is in heaviness. But not so was it with the pure-hearted, the refined Ruth Allen. She thanked Heaven that when all was darkness and desolation within, she could look abroad upon a world of light and beauty ; that when earthly love had deceived her, she could cast herself still on the bosom of One whose love and compassion are infinite. She saw the lily that, without care or labor, was so richly clothed ; the wanton birds who were so tenderly sheltered and sustained ; the lowing herds trampling down their abundant provision in field and meadow ; and she raised her earnest eyes to heaven, whispering, in childlike faith, " Father, wilt thou not much more care for

me and mine?"   And think you that the young
wife and mother pleaded in vain?   Never.   "If
ye, being evil, know how to give good gifts unto
your children, how much more shall your Father
which is in heaven give good things unto them
that ask him?"

While Ruth Allen was yet speaking, her
prayer was answered.   A solemn providence,
which deprived an evil associate of life in a
moment, roused the sleeping conscience of her
husband.   God spoke, and he was reclaimed.
As a humble penitent he sought mercy of
Heaven, and forgiveness of her whose young
hopes he had so cruelly blighted.   Old things
with him were passed away, and all things become new.   God smiled abundantly on the labor
of their hands.   The showers fell freely, and
the sun lay long upon their meadows;   their
flocks multiplied in the pasture, and their cattle
in the stall.   They now had bread enough and to
spare;   and she whose eyes had faded by stitch-
ing wearily over the dull midnight lamp, patch-
ing the rags of her children, had now the joy of
seeing them comfortably and decently clothed.
Her grateful heart was full to overflowing.   God

had given her more of temporal good than her humble spirit had ever craved. He alone knoweth how much of this earthly good was given in approbation of her affectionate trust in Him.

"But shall a man receive good at the hand of the Lord, and not evil?" No; for "the day of prosperity and the day of adversity are set one over against the other." While the long-deserted home was beginning to bud and blossom like a rose, the angel of death sped thither and overshadowed their dwelling with his dark wing. The first-born, who had been his mother's stay, who had sympathized in her anguish, kissed away her tears, and whispered, "Wait a while, mother; in thirteen short years I'll be a man, and then you shall never suffer any more;"—he, the child of her love and her sorrow, was taken away, and his place left vacant in the little bed, at the board, and at the hearthstone. She had then no time for tears—her care was all for the other two, who, while their brother slept in peace, were tossing in burning fevers on their bed of pain. The second, and then the third, in one short week, were laid beside him in the little graveyard of the new settlement; and the home of Ruth Allen, which so lately had rung with the merry laughter of three noble boys, was left unto her desolate. How desolate, bereaved mothers only can know. Did she not wrap herself in deep gloom, and weep as one who would not be comforted, when this great calamity befell her? No; she *gave* her sons to God—they were not *torn* from her. So far from charging God foolishly, she even thanked him that, while many wretched mothers were weeping over ruined sons, she had the assurance that her whole family were folded forever in the bosom of Infinite Love,—secure from hunger, neglect, temptation, and pain. Then, when this free-will offering had been made to Heaven, did she, with a chastened mien, go abroad among the poor and vicious, seeking for children to fill the places thus made vacant. During the ten years that followed, four nameless little ones were received into her family and her heart. What had once been a forest settlement was fast changing into the metropolis of a growing State. Wealth flowed in upon farmer Allen, by the sale of his rich lands. Servants and laborers filled their house and grounds, and

12*

to all of them his wife was as a mother. She addressed each dependent as " child," and they were constrained to believe that in all her deal-ings she had their welfare at heart. Then she began to be called " our misthress, dear sowl," and then the neighbors and friends, and finally everybody, called her " Mother Allen, dear soul." A rude emigrant, all unused to such gentle tones as hers, exclaimed, after being a week or two beneath her roof, " Sure, I thought afoor I coom to this hoose that Protestants were all like wild bastes. I was taught by my moother—rest her sowl!—that not a fut of thim hiritics could iver inter hiven, unless they first coom into the hooly moother choorch. But if that same is thrue, it's meself would rather be after living forever with the likes of my misthress, dear sowl, than in hiven itself, among my own coonthry folk ; for it's drinking and fighting they be foriver, when there be so many of thims togither, and not a Protestant at all there to separate thim and make pace. Och, och, but there's hivin in her eyes— my misthress, dear sowl ! "

Mother Allen had her trials among the many working people her husband employed. Her confidence was often abused, and her disinterested love repaid with black ingratitude. But through all she remained the same. No ear ever heard her taunt these rude children of oppression with their foreign birth, their early poverty, their false religion. She reasoned with them as human beings, she entreated them *for their own sakes*, and wooed them back to duty by her patient efforts. Many a lady, reared in a home of elegance, might have learned lessons of dignity and propriety from Mother Allen, in her intercourse with and management of her servants. In no way is the true lady more readily distinguished from the counterfeit than in her deportment towards these humble members of her family.

The love of this dear woman began at home, but it did not end there. The sufferer everywhere found in her a friend, the erring and fallen a mother and an encouraging counsellor. In her closet, at her fireside, over her work, among her neighbors, in the church of God, everywhere, it was evident that she lived not unto herself. The most hardened scoffer was forced to admit that she was a bright and shining light, a beautiful example for the wives and mothers around her. The law of kindness was ever on her tongue, and the gentlest and tenderest rebuke ready on her lip. Many a youth, who had scorned a father's counsel and despised a mother's eutreaties, won by the affectionate interest and sweet tones of Mother Allen, has listened respectfully to her earnest warning, and been drawn by her efforts to forsake the seat of the scorner and to seek God's house.

But the place where this good woman's influence was the most deeply felt—and it was a place she coveted—was at the bed of pain. The young, who, having been often reproved, had hardened their hearts, would call for her in the hour of their souls' extremity. "O," cried one such, "I cannot look upon my afflicted father, I cannot see the pastor,—his face would only remind me of the many warnings I have received unheeded from his lips. But bring Mother Allen to me. I can almost see 'hope' now in the memory of her dear face. Let her come and teach me—let her come, *and, with her faith*, pray for me."

But the frosts of age fell upon her; its infirmities bound her fast, so that she could no longer go about doing good. But when she could not go out to her work, the work came in to her. The winter of her life had no long, dark days, no listless melancholy, no fretful murmurings. She moved around her house in a wheel-chair, demanding little care, but receiving much,—the object of a thousand little acts of delicate love, which money could never purchase. A domestic, being asked if she were not weary, replied, "No; I'm never weary in waiting upon *her*, for her patience would shame me, if I were."

Mother Allen had learned that most beautiful lesson for woman, how to " grow old gracefully." She was not only borne with, but she was really admired for her age, and the charms that clustered around it. Life's sun, which had been so often concealed by clouds, had its setting in a calm, bright sky. We may almost say of her that she never died, her going was so like sinking into a quiet sleep. It was one cold, bright day in winter that she entered into her rest. Her chair had been drawn to the western window, that she might use the last of daylight in finishing one of several little garments for a suffering family. The last stitch was set, the last button sewed on, her thimble was placed on the window-seat, and the spectacles lay in her hand. She was noticed gazing at the gorgeous sunset, whose splendor was reflected upon snow and ice-clothed trees, making the whole scene like a world of diamonds. The cheerful bell rang for tea; her aged companion and her attendant came to draw her chair into the dining-room Each took an arm of it, when her husband said, "She is asleep, dear soul!" It was the sleep that knows no waking. She was not, for God had taken her. —*J. D. C.*

THE FRUITFUL CHRISTIAN'S END.

WHEN in the evening, after a hot day, one returns to his home laden with fruit, all the dwellers rejoice. Thus I see thee, thou pure, blessed spirit, enter into thy Father's home, and the dwellers in heaven rejoice.—*Tholuck.*

SUFFERING WITH CHRIST.

SHALL I not be ashamed of the roses around my brow, when I see Him, and all the princes of his kingdom, with the crown of thorns?—*Tholuck.*

THE SYMPATHY OF JESUS.

WHEN two persons meet who are able to re-count similar necessities, and the same buffet-ings of Satan, O, what mutual disclosures take place! what trustful communicativeness, what tender sympathy, is then manifest! Then one soul gushes out and flows over into the other, and time steals rapidly on. But, on the other hand, toward one who knows not our needs by experience, we are dumb, reserved, and take no pleasure in communicating, because we fear that he will be able neither to understand nor sympa-thize with us.

So, indeed, would we have 'kept further away from our heavenly Friend, had he not become our companion in tribulation. But now the thought is exceedingly refreshing, that he him-self was tempted in all points like as we are, and knows the bitterest anguish of our soul from his own experience. Now, even though no fel-low-man understands us, ah! still we know there is yet one Friend at hand, to whom we need but lisp a word of our affairs and concerns, and he at once comprehends all we feel. His experience reaches down into the thickest nights of the soul—into the most frightful depths of inward sufferings or conflicts.

Under no juniper-tree canst thou sit, which has not overshadowed him ; no thorn can wound thee, from which his heart has not bled ; no fiery dart can hit thee, which has not been shot at his sacred head. He can indeed have compassion. Yes, only believe it, dear soul; as often as thou liest in the furnace, over thee the eyes of the watchful Refiner melt in tears, and a great, holy mother-heart bleeds for thee in sympathy from heaven.—*Krummacher.*

MY GRANDMOTHER.

WHAT tender recollections cluster round thy name, cherished friend of our childhood days ! How quickly the name of grandmother reaches our ears, leading us far back into the half-forgotten past, when we all, light-hearted and free, sat at her feet. O, blissful hours they were— all too bright, too gladsome, to be lasting ! Yes, the hours spent at grandma's home shed a bright halo over the present. Her home was

not one to attract a stranger; there were no
costly displays of architecture, no vine-festooned
bowers, but simply a little farm-house, that ever
created emotions of beauty in my young heart.
Methinks I see it now, as when I last visited it
before she was called to her last, long sleep,—
with the old well-sweep that seemed to vie with
the towering elm at its side, the brook that
flowed gently o'er its pebbly bed, on, on, down
to the rustic old mill, whose "rafters have all
tumbled in," and the orchard that reached far
along the hillside—even to the silent city of the
dead. Oft had I wandered there *alone* among
the mounds, with thoughtful heart; and now—
tread lightly, speak softly, for do ye not see
that "short and narrow bed," newly made, and
will ye not ask Heaven's blessing upon the
household band that have been made desolate?

Ah, well do I remember the beautiful smile
that lighted up my grandma's brow, as she welcomed me, as oft before, to her humble home!
I thought the wrinkles had deepened upon her
brow, the light faded from her eye,—but still
reflecting more of heaven than when she last
gave me a parting blessing. She seemed more

thoughtful, as she sat there, in the "old arm-chair," with the family Bible upon the stand by her side, than I had seen her before ; and oftener spoke of heaven and its joys, oftener wished me to read to her from her most precious earthly treasure, the Bible.

Tell me not of "duties to the aged," but rather of the peaceful pleasure one receives in performing acts of kindness to them. Ah, speak kindly, lovingly, to them, for

> Enough of sorrow this cold world hath,
> Enough of care in its later path.

Then see that ye add not a furrow to the sil-vered brow of the feeble and aged one.   Yes,

> "Speak gently to age !
> A weary way is the rough and toilsome road of life,
> As one by one its joys decay,
> And its hopes go out 'mid its lengthened strife."

Never have I regretted one kind word spoken to my dear grandmother ; but a sigh oft swells my bosom, and tears moisten my eye, because I so poorly smoothed her rough and toilsome path. Death claimed our loved one when the lamp of life was almost extinguished.   She is now lying under those brown autumn leaves, with the sad winds blowing across her grave, and her pure spirit has gone to that land where age dims not the eye. Death to her was but the commencement of life—a passport to a brighter world, where dwell many who have gone on before, and await her in their eternal home. May we all be gathered, at last, to join her in singing praises to Him who sitteth upon the throne!—*Rural New Yorker.*

I HAVE gained the victory, and Christ is holding out both hands to embrace me.—*Rutherford.*

A WORD FOR THE UNMARRIED.

A FINISHED life—a life which has made the best of all the materials granted to it, and through which, be its web dark or bright, its pattern clear or clouded, can now be traced plainly the hand of the Great Designer—surely this is worth living for! And, though at its end it may be somewhat lonely; though a servant, and not a daughter's arm may guide the failing step; though most likely it will be strangers only who come about the dying bed, close the eyes that no husband ever kissed, and draw the shroud kindly over the poor, withered breast, where no child's head has ever lain ; still such a life is not to be pitied, for it is a complete life.   It has fulfilled its appointed course, and returns to the Giver of all breath.   Nor will He forget it when He counteth up his jewels.— *Chambers' Journal.*

HEAVEN NEAR.

One should go to sleep at night as homesick passengers do, saying, Perhaps in the morning we shall see the shore.   To us who are Christians, it is not a solemn, but a delightful thought, that perhaps nothing but the opaque bodily eye prevents us from beholding the gate which is open just before us, and nothing but the dull ear prevents us from hearing the ringing of those bells of joy which welcome us to the heavenly land.—*H. W. Beecher.*

HEAVEN.

As, though the sky is not steadfastly clear, but often is covered with clouds, yet through the folds there shine at intervals the everlasting stars, so through the darkness of our hearts there steals at times the celestial glory, and we rejoice that there is a heaven above the world. —*H W. Beecher.*

HUMILITY.

THE bird that soars on highest wing
    Builds on the ground her lowly nest;
And she that doth most sweetly sing
    Sings in the shade when all things rest;
    In lark and nightingale we see
    What honor hath humility.

When Mary chose the " better part,"
    She meekly sat at Jesus' feet;
And Lydia's gently-opened heart
    Was made for God's own temple meet;
    Fairest and best adorned is she
    Whose clothing is humility.

The saint that wears heaven's brightest crown
    In deepest adoration bends;
The weight of glory bows him down
    Then most when most his soul ascends;
    Nearest the throne itself must be
    The footstool of humility.

James Montgomery.

GOD'S MERCY.

No mercy hath been more endeared than what hath broken out of the thickest cloud, or more full and sweet than what hath come after much patience and continued wrestlings.—*Fleming.*

TRUST IN GOD.

Nothing does so much establish the mind, amidst the rolling and turbulence of present things, as both a look above them, and a look beyond them : above them, to the steady and good Hand by which they are ruled; and beyond them, to the sweet and beautiful end to which, by that Hand, they shall be brought.—*Leighton.*

CHILDHOOD.

Childhood often holds a truth, with its feeble fingers, which the grasp of manhood cannot retain, which it is the pride of utmost age to recover.—*Ruskin.*

GOD'S INFINITY.

The infinity of God is not mysterious, it is only unfathomable ; not concealed, but incomprehensible.   It is a clear infinity, the darkness of the pure, unsearchable sea.—*Ruskin.*

CHRIST EVERYWHERE.

WHEN a native female Christian of India was interrogated as to the state of her mind, she replied, "Happy! happy! I have Christ *here*," laying her hand on her Bengáli Bible; "and Christ *here*," pressing it to her heart; "and Christ *there*," pointing toward heaven.

EVENING–TIME.

ZECH. XIV. 7.

AT evening-time let there be light :—
　Life's little day draws near its close ;
Around me fall the shades of night,—
　The night of death, the grave's repose.
　To crown my joys, to end my woes,
At evening-time let there be light.

At evening-time let there be light :—
　Stormy and dark hath been my day ;
Yet rose the morn oenignly bright,
　Dews, birds, and flowers, cheered all the way.
　O, for one sweet, one parting ray !
At evening-time let there be light.

At evening-time there *shall* be light,
  For God hath said, "So let it be."
Fear, doubt, and anguish, take their flight,—
  His glory now is risen on me!
  Mine eyes shall his salvation see;—
'T is evening-time, and there *is* light.

             James Montgomery.

THE SINNER'S SAVIOUR.

KNEELING by the bed of an apparently dying saint, I said, " Well, sister, He has been precious to you ; you can rejoice in his covenant mercies, and his past loving-kindnesses." She put out her hand, and said, " Ah, sir, do not talk about them now ; I want the sinner's Saviour as much now as ever. It is not a saint's Saviour I want ; it is still a sinner's Saviour that I am in need of, for I am a sinner still."—*Spurgeon.*

MEMBERS ONE OF ANOTHER.

THE individuals of each race of lower animals, being not intended to hold among each other those relations of charity which are the privilege of humanity, are not adapted to each other's assistance, admiration, or support, by differences of power and function. But the love of the human race is increased by their individual differences, and the unity of the creature made perfect by each having something to bestow and to receive; bound to the rest by a thousand various necessities and various gratitudes, humility in each rejoicing to admire in his fellow that which he finds not in himself, and each being in some respect the complement of his race.—*Ruskin.*

THE BEAUTIFUL IN THE GOOD.

THERE is not any virtue the exercise of which, even momentarily, will not impress a new fairness on the features.—*Ruskin.*

SPIRITUAL BEAUTY.

THERE is a certain period of the soul-culture when it begins to interfere with some of the characters of typical beauty belonging to the bodily frame, the stirring of the intellect wearing down the flesh, and the moral enthusiasm burning its way out to heaven, through the emaciation of the earthen vessel; and there is, in this indication of subduing the mortal by the immortal part, an ideal glory of perhaps a purer and higher range than that of the more perfect material form. We conceive, I think, more nobly of the weak presence of Paul, than of the fair and ruddy countenance of David.—*Ruskin.*

VANITY OF LIFE.

I HAVE seen all that society can show, and enjoyed all that wealth can give me, and I am satisfied that much is vanity, if not vexation of spirit.—*Walter Scott.*

SONG OF THE AGED.

" Now, also, when I am old and gray-headed, O God, forsake me not ; until I have showed thy strength unto this generation, and thy power to every one that is to come."—Ps. lxxi. 18.

WITH years oppressed, with sorrows worn,
Dejected, harassed, sick, forlorn,
To thee, O God, I pray ;
To thee my withered hands arise ;
To thee I lift my failing eyes ;
O, cast me not away !

Thy mercy heard my infant prayer ;
Thy love, with all a mother's care,
Sustained my childish days ;

Thy goodness watched my ripening youth,
And formed my heart to love thy truth,
   And filled my lips with praise.

O, Saviour! has thy grace declined?
Can years affect the Eternal mind,
   Or time its love decay?
A thousand ages pass thy sight,
And all their long and weary flight
   Is gone like yesterday.

Then, even in age and grief, thy name
Shall still my languid heart inflame,
   And bow my faltering knee;
O, yet this bosom feels the fire;
This trembling hand and drooping lyre
   Have yet a strain for thee.

Yes, broken, tuneless, still, O Lord,
This voice, transported, shall record
   Thy goodness, tried so long,
Till, sinking slow, with calm decay,
Its feeble murmurs melt away
   Into a seraph's song.—*Grant.*

DEATH OF JOHN FOSTER.

THE substantial peace which he had attained
did not desert him in his dying hours. As he
felt his strength gradually stealing away, he

remarked on his increasing weakness, and added,
' But I can pray, and that is a glorious thing."
Truly a glorious thing, to look up to an Omnipotent Father ! to speak to him—to love him—to
stretch upward as a babe from the cradle, that
he may lift his child in his everlasting arms to
the resting-place of his own bosom.   This is the
portion of the dying Christian.   He was over-
heard thus speaking with himself : " ' O death,
where is thy sting ? O grave, where is thy victory? Thanks be to God, who giveth us the
victory,   through   our   Lord   Jesus   Christ.' "
—*Bayne.*

I AM LIKE A BROKEN VESSEL.

PS. XXXI. 12.

Cast as a broken vessel by,
    Thy will I can no longer do ;
Yet, while a daily death I die,
    Thy power I may in weakness show ;
My patience may thy glory raise,
My speechless woe proclaim thy praise.

Mrs. Steele.

AGED BELIEVERS.

Aged and mellow saints have **so** sweet a savor
of Christ in them, that their conversation is like

streams from Lebanon, sweetly refreshing to him who delights to hear of the glories of redeeming love. They have tried the anchor in the hour of storm, they have tested the armor in the day of battle, they have proved the shadow of the great rock in the burning noontide in the weary land; therefore do they talk of those things, and of *Him* who is all these unto them, with an unction and a relish which we who have but just put on our harness can enjoy, although we cannot attain unto it at present. We must dive into the same waters, if we would bring up the same pearls.—*Spurgeon.*

THE DEATH OF A CHRISTIAN MERCHANT, SAMUEL BUDGETT.

I like to hear of the beauties of heaven, but I do not dwell upon them. No, what I rejoice in is, that Christ will be there. Where He is, there shall I be also. I know that He is in me, and I in Him. I shall see Him as He is. I delight in knowing that.

I have sunk into the arms of Omnipotent love. I am going the way of all flesh; but, bless God, I'm ready. I trust in the merits of

my Redeemer. I care not when, or where, or
how ; glory be to God !—*Bayne.*

THE BORDER-LAND.

FATHER, into thy loving hands
  My feeble spirit I commit,
While wandering in these Border-lands,
  Until thy voice shall summon it.

Father, I would not dare to choose
  A longer life, an earlier death;
I know not what my soul might lose
  By shortened or protracted breath.

These Border-lands are calm and still,
  And solemn are their silent shades;
And my heart welcomes them, until
  The light of life's long evening fades.

I heard them spoken of with dread,
  As fearful and unquiet places;
Shades where the living and the dead
  Look sadly in each other's faces;

But since thy hand hath led me here,
  And I have seen the Border-land,—
Seen the dark river flowing near,
  Stood on its brink, as now I stand,—

There has been nothing to alarm
　My trembling soul; how could I fear
While thus encircled with thine arm?—
　I never felt thee half so near!

What should appall me in a place
　That brings me hourly nearer thee?
Where I may almost see thy face,—
　Surely 'tis here my soul would be!

They say thy waves are dark and deep,—
　That Faith hath perished in the river;
They speak of death with fear, and weep;
　Shall my soul perish?—Never, never!

I know that thou wilt never leave
　The soul that trembles while it clings
To thee; I know thou wilt achieve
　Its passage on thine outstretched wings

I cannot see the golden gate
　Unfolding yet to welcome me;
I cannot yet anticipate
　The joy of heaven's jubilee;

But I will calmly watch and pray,
　Until I hear my Saviour's voice
Calling my happy soul away,
　To see his glory, and rejoice.

A PARTING WORD.

"The Eternal God is thy refuge, and underneath are the Everlasting arms."

WHAT more can you desire, afflicted believer? No frail and crumbling tabernacle, no mere human friend, is declared to be thy refuge. It is none other than the Eternal God, who is from everlasting to everlasting, the same yesterday, to-day, and forever. It is He who invites you to run into his arms, and be forever safe.

But do you say, I am so feeble, so utterly without strength, that I cannot run to him, or make any movement toward him? Then see, further, how he has provided for you. "*Underneath* you are the everlasting arms." All you need to do is just to yield yourself up to be sustained by those arms. Sink into them ; they are already beneath you—they even now support you. Let childlike faith banish your fears ; rest you in the arms of the Eternal God. Lie there as a child, in your Father's loving, all-encompassing embrace. Those "arms" cannot be palsied or too heavily burdened, and so let go their hold ; they are "everlasting." They bear up the universe ; surely, they can sustain *you.* Millions have there found a blessed, an unfailing refuge and rest. Believe their testimony—rather, believe God's own word of promise. There you *are*, O tried believer! those everlasting arms *are* underneath you, though sometimes you see them not. There we leave you.—FAREWELL!

Tommy's Prayer.

DURING the years I was at work in the slums of southeast London, writes Philip I. Roberts, the following example of a simple faith came to my knowledge: A poor little slum child of about eleven developed a malady which demanded an instant operation. He was taken to Guy's Hospital, where the great doctor who examined him had to tell him that there was ju a fighting chance for his life.

The seats of the operating theatre, rising tier above tier like the gallery of a church. were filled with long rows of students who had come to witness the greatest surgeon of his time use the knife. The little patient was brought in and, during some preliminaries, placed in a cushioned chair. Looking around at the great throng of men, he said timidly to one of the assistant doctors: "Please, sir, I should be very glad if one of you gentlemen would say just a little prayer for me."

There was a profound silence. Nobody moved, so the little slum child knelt down and said: "Dear Jesus, I'm only a poor, weak, little lad, but, please, I'd like to live. So, dear Jesus, please help this kind gentleman. so that he shall do his work right. Amen." Having said that, the boy climbed on the table and lay back with a smile lighting up his face.

The great surgeon stood at the head of the table, fully aware that he was about to perform an operation that would test his skill to the utmost. For a moment or so he was visibly agitated. The students exchanged glances. Never had they seen their chief unnerved before, and this condition now augured but ill for the life of the waif. Yet as he looked on the still moving lips of the prostrate boy, a great calm stole over the doctor. He commenced to operate, and immediately realized that the slum child's prayer was being answered. Coolness of head, steadiness of hand and delicacy of touch all came as they were needed. The boy's life hung on a mere thread, but the skillful surgeon did not snap it.

Next morning the surgeon stood in the
ward by the bedside of his little patient.
Taking his hand he said: "Well, Tommy,
Jesus heard your prayer yesterday."   A
confident smile lit up the boy's face as
he answered: "I knew He would."   Then
his features clouded over, and he said:
"You were very good to me, too, doctor.
And I have nothing to give—nothing at
all."   Then a happy thought came to him
and his face lit up again, and he whispered: "But I can keep on praying to Jesus
for you, can't I?"   A great lump came into
the doctor's throat.   "That you can," he
answered huskily, "and that will be better
than any sort of money, for God knows
I need the prayers of one like you!"—
Presbyterian Banner.

I think that is true in so far as the love
deepens and enriches our spiritual life.   In
regard to unanswered prayer a beautiful
thought is expressed in a favorite hymn of
mine :

Unanswered yet? The prayer your lips have
    pleaded
  In agony of heart these many years?
Does faith begin to fail? Is hope departing?
  And think you all in vain those falling tears?
Say not the Father hath not heard your prayer:
You shall have your desire some time, somewhere.

Unanswered yet? tho' when you first presented
  This one petition at the Father's throne,
It seemed you could not wait the time of asking
  So urgent was your heart to make it known:
Tho' years have passed since then, do not despair;
The Lord will answer you sometime, somewhere.

Unanswered yet? Faith cannot be unanswered;
  Her feet are firmly planted on the Rock.
Amid the wildest storms she stands undaunted,
  Nor quails before the loudest thunder-shock.
She knows Omnipotence has heard her prayer,
And cries, "It shall be done" sometime, somewhere.

HOPEFUL.

GOD BE WITH YOU.

God be with you till we meet
  again,
    By his counsels guide, uphold
    you,
    With his sheep securely fold
    you,
God be with you till we meet
  again.

CHORUS.

  Till we meet, till we meet,
  Till we meet at Jesus' feet ;
  Till we meet, till we meet,
God be with you till we meet
  again.

God be with you till we meet
  again,
    'Neath his wings securely hide
    you ;
    Daily manna still provide you,
God be with you till we meet
  again.

God be with you till we meet
  again,
    When life's perils thick con-
    found you ;
    Put his loving around you,
God be with you till we meet
  again.

God be with you till we meet
  again,
    Keep love's banner floating
    o'er you,
    Smite death's threat'ning wave
    before you,
God be with you till we meet
  again.

***

At the Thanksgiving Fire.

    We are all here !
      Father, mother,
      Sister, brother,
    All who hold each other dear ;
Each chair is filled, we're all at home.
To-night let no dissension come ;
It is not often thus around
Our old familiar hearth we're found.
Bless, then, the meeting and the spot ;
For once be every care forgot ;
Let gentle peace assert her power,
And kind affection rule the hour.
    We're all, all here !
        —CHARLES SPRAGUE.

"Keep the memory sacred of her prayer
for you, and read her Book;" and thus the
prayer was answered.

"Uplands," the beautiful home became
more beautiful—consecrated to the service
of the Lord Jesus Christ. There, many
weary ones found rest; wanderers were reclaimed; and sinners learned of Him who
'taketh away the sin of the world." Ger-
trude Burleigh never forgot that evening
after the storm, when, seized with fear, her
father recalled a gracious memory which
revealed a Saviour through the world of
God, according to her mother's words and
prayer.

Unanswered yet, the prayer your lips have
        pleaded,
    In agony of heart these many years?
Does faith begin to fail; is hope departing,
    And think you all in vain those falling
        tears?
Say not the Father had not heard your
        prayer;
You shall have your desire some time, some-
        where.

—London Christian.

The Value of Kind Words

To the Home Circle: Kind words will live in our minds while life shall last. How sweet is the memory of the kind words spoken by friends now far from us. They help cheer us on life's way. If we are rich or poor we can speak kind words to make the road onward brighter. I never have known any good to come from unkind words.

Then let us all speak kind words—the old and the young. In that way we will accomplish much good, and help the world to grow better.

Kind words and thoughts that come from the heart are sweeter than music to one, and I am sure they are to others.

We have the opportunity almost every day to speak a kind word to someone. Our next door neighbor may need a kind word of cheer. The student may need a word of encouragement or help. It is a great thought for young people to start out in life with a determination to live a useful life. They will succeed if they have a pleasant face and a kind word for everyone. · Mrs. Lucy M. Mellen.

Testimony and Petition

Dear Praying Ones: I wish to ask the brothers and sisters of the Hom. Circle to pray earnestly that I may receive health and strength, both spiritually and physically. Also that another thing which bothers me greatly may never come to pass. Please pray that the Lord will guide and di-